I0748347

THE MARRIAGE CLAIM

REIGNING HEARTS

EVIE MITCHELL

THUNDER THIGHS PUBLISHING

This book is a work of fiction. Names, characters, places, incidents, facts, sometimes random sentences are either the product of the author's imagination or are used in what she hopes is an entirely flattering but fictitious manner. Any resemblance to actual persons, living or dead, or actual events, locales is entirely coincidental.

Copyright © 2021 by Hendrix House Pty Ltd, on behalf of author Evie Mitchell; All rights reserved.

No part of this book may be distributed, posted, or reproduced in any form by digital or mechanical means, including via TikTok, Instagram, Facebook or Twitter, without prior written permission of the publisher.

Editor: Nicole Wilson, Evermore Editing
http://www.evermoreediting.wixsite.com/info
Cover: Laras Putri

ACKNOWLEDGEMENT OF COUNTRY

I acknowledge the Traditional Custodians of the lands on which I write, the Ngunnawal people, and pay my respect to elders both past and present.

I acknowledge the continued and deep spiritual relationship of the Australian Aboriginal and Torres Strait Islander peoples' to this land, and their unique cultural and spiritual relationships to the land, waters and seas and their rich contribution to society.

Always was, always will be.

AUTHOR NOTE

My Dearest Greedy Reader,

Thank you for choosing to read The Marriage Claim!

Trigger warnings are listed as follows: Misogyny, attempted assassination, attempted assault, privacy violation, shipwreck trauma, discussion of death, dirty talk, consensual sex, claiming wife, trust issues.

If you have any concerns, please email me at EvieMitchellAuthor@gmail.com.

THE MARRIAGE CLAIM

"As the warrior who saved your life, I ask for the right to invoke the akaternok ah yalonel—the Marriage Claim."

I have no choice but to marry. I need an heir—for the good of the country and the continuation of my bloodline.

If I could, I'd do it alone. But as Queen, I need a consort—and the only option is for me to take a husband.

Jonathan is completely unsuitable. Charming, powerful, attractive—and vying to be our country's next Prime Minister. He's a terrible choice.

But when he saves my life and requests akaternok ah yalonel—the Marriage Claim—I'm left with the hardest decision of my life.

Does he want my heart... or my crown?

PROLOGUE

Katherine
Astipia Kingdom
King's Bedchamber,
The Royal Palace

I sat by my father's bed, watching as his breathing labored, the soft beeping of the heart monitor becoming an uneven rhythm.

I could no longer deny reality, no longer hide behind hope and determined, willful ignorance— my father was dying.

On the other side of the bed sat my mother, my brother, and sister. Each stoic, alternating between watching my father and stealing stricken glances towards me. Around the bed stood a gathering of observers. Men and women, some medical staff, some religious, some simply there to observe the legality of this moment. All intrusive and unwanted, they were a violation on this private, devastating moment.

The price we pay even in our final moments.

An hour, a moment, a lifetime later—too soon and much too late— my father's breath changed. A terrible crackling gargle escaping his gasping mouth. Across the bed, my sister placed her hand in my mother's, a silent vulnerable search for reassurance. In turn, my mother reached out to my brother, gripping his hand tightly.

I met Leo's gaze, my back stiffening, determination straightening my spine. He nodded once, his face stoic as he patted our mother's hand, squeezing it tight.

I was glad for her, that she had them to provide comfort. On my side of the bed, I alone had to bear witness to this moment. No hands to hold, no comfort available.

The head surgeon pressed a stethoscope to my father's chest, listening.

"It's known as a death rattle," he explained, tucking the scope away. "I can assure you, he won't feel any pain but his time is near."

I gave him a nod, reaching out to capture my father's hand, bringing down towards me, determined to hold on to him until the end. His hand felt clammy, his fingers twitching between my own. I wished my grip could anchor him to me, to this world.

I'm not ready for you to leave. I still need you.

The end came quicker than I'd thought and yet longer than I'd wished. An hour, perhaps two, and then the horrible crackling sound suddenly ended, my father's chest decompressing fully, never to rise again.

Machines began to wail, the surgeon moving quickly to switch it off, then pressed fingers to his carotid artery, gaze fixed on his wrist watch. With ice in my veins, I pressed my thumb to father's pulse, feeling the last beats of his heart as he left this world.

One.
Two.
One.
Two.
One.
One.
One.
Father?

I pressed my thumb harder against his skin, searching for that second beat.

You've left me. I'm alone. Father....

"Time of death, nine oh three a.m." The doctor declared, looking to the gathered crowd.

I closed my eyes for a moment, sucking in a stiff breath.

It's done. Be brave. Do him proud.

I opened my eyes, raising my head to see my mother staring at me from across the bed, tears silently falling down her beautiful face. My sister pressed a handkerchief to her eyes, her shoulders shaking with silent sobs as my brother stared, glassy-eyed at our father's lifeless body.

A stifled sob broke the silence of the room.

I turned my dry gaze to the gathering, seeing tears and devastation written across every face.

The Prime Minister stepped forward, bowing his head.

"The King is dead, long live the Queen."

"Long live the Queen."

The words were echoed by the gathered, each dropping into a curtsey or a bow. Even my mother and siblings stood, only to drop before me, their heads bowed in respect.

I rose, pressing one last kiss to my father's hand. Placing it gently on his chest, then smoothing the blanket that covered him.

His eyes were shut but I didn't need to see them to know he had left this burdensome place. Already his face showed signs that his soul had gone. The pain that had plagued him for years had been wiped clean, his skin slack, his muscles waning.

"Good bye, My King." I whispered the words just for him. "Farewell, Father."

Straightening, forcing steel into my spine I turned to the gathered.

"Thank you for observing the vigil," I told them, locking my emotions into a tiny box. "The arrangements have been made. My family will retire to our residence." I looked to the press secretary. "I trust you'll post the notice?"

He nodded, tears glistening in his eyes. "As you wish... Your Majesty."

The words, the first spoken to me in my new role, settled responsibility like a weight upon my shoulders, the mantel heavy and unfamiliar. A role for which I have been raised, curated, and tutored my whole life. And yet with this moment upon me I felt ill equipped and overwhelmed. A duty that passed to me only through the death of another.

My father.

With a mental shake, I shoved away any

anxiety or fear, determined to present nothing but strength and determination—despite my overwhelming grief.

I am Queen. Long may I reign.

Gods help us all.

1

———

KATHERINE

Formal Meeting Room, The Royal Palace
Two years later

"No."

"Your Majesty, please—"

I pressed hands to the table as I glared down the length of it at the men attempting to control my life.

"I said, no." I repeated, my tone ice.

"The crown carries a price, my Queen."

Everything in me revolted. Anger warring with despair.

"You must see," the Prime Minister said, spreading his hands in supplication. "The people have allowed you to grieve. But two years without an heir... it's unheard of."

"Not since your many great grandfather, King—"

"Leopold the Third. I know my family history." I waved a dismissive hand, fighting to restrain my anger.

I sucked in a breath, forcing myself to casually lean back, to settle into my throne. I knit my fingers, bringing them to my chin, adopting the same pensive pose my father had used throughout his reign. I did so deliberately, finding over the past two years that it had reassured the men in the room, eliciting an emotional response, the ghost of my father a memory I had yet to shake.

Manipulation, thy name is Katherine.

I lowered my hands, glancing up at the men. "Prime Minister, explain your reasoning."

If the polls were correct, he wouldn't be sitting in this room come September. The people were displeased with his performance—he promised much but delivered little and most to the benefit of the rich.

His term had started under my father and I'd be pleased to see him gone. He wore far too much cologne, rarely said anything of value, and spoke down to every woman in his vicinity — especially his Queen. I'd been forced more than once to put him in his place. Gently, of course. It wouldn't do to have conflict between the head of state and the people's elected official.

I reigned over a constitutional monarchy, where power between the crown and the executive was a tenuous balance of diplomacy and negotiations. I may have final power, but my ability to govern relied upon the will of parliament bringing forward the proposals I wished to endorse.

And this Prime Minister? He'd brought forth nothing but half-hearted rubbish for me to consider. Twice in my short two-year reign I'd been forced to send motions back to Parliament for renegotiation, the Bills insufficient to provide for my people. The last time such an event had occurred ad been two decades ago, under my father. That I'd reject not one but two had left him red-faced and resentful.

I'd known the Prime Minister disliked me. I hadn't quite realised how he wished to control me until this moment.

An ambush. I'd walked into a goddamned ambush.

"As you are aware, Your Majesty," the Prime Minister began, wringing his hands nervously. "The constitutions requires that you name an heir within four years of ascending the throne. With your sister engaged to a foreigner, and your brother...." He paused and I found myself curious if he would finally discuss my brother's sexual preference.

I'd long ago found that men like the Prime Minister saw any threat to what they thought as 'the right way to live life' as insurmountable—and I knew my brother's sexuality, no matter how ordinary and normal, would be met with disapproval by this worm of a man.

He proved me right when he cleared his throat, avoiding discussing Leo's sexuality by saying, "Serving overseas. Which would put him in great danger. I see no other option. You must marry."

I raised an eyebrow at the rest of the table. "And does the table agree?"

The Archbishop cleared his throat. "It's prudent to at least consider the option, Ma'am."

You knew this day would come, Kit.

I couldn't lie to myself. This moment had been brewing for years. I bordered on thirty, my fertility now rife speculation in the media. My life had already been dissected, my virginity questioned time and again by conservative gossip rags, feminists determined to see a progressive queen on the throne. My sexuality, much like the rest of me, remained open speculation.

I was a progressive, I made no secret of that. But my private life, the scraps of it that remained, were mine. In the privacy of my bedroom, locked away from prying eyes and open ears, I remained free. Free to rage, free to cry, free to love.

Well, I had experienced two of those three. And that was the problem. It wasn't that I didn't wish for love, I did. For all my practicality I remained a closet romantic, stealing romance novels from my sister, wishing for the day I'd experience the spark that let me know I'd found my one.

But when you were Queen few people approached you without an ulterior motive. Even the most genuine of my friends, those I had thought were close companions, near and dear to my heart, had capitalised on my name. I counted those close to me on one hand, and of that number only two were not related to me by blood or marriage.

Fame and fortune were fleeting, royalty was forever. And I'd learned the hard way that no one truly understood this, not even my siblings. Only my father had understood this burden.

And he's gone.

"Thank you," I said, finally rising from my seat. The men rose with me, all deference and meekness now.

Bastards.

"I'll consider your words."

I walked to the door, then paused, turning slightly. "And Prime Minister?"

He straightened. "Ma'am?"

I offered him a small smile. "I expect you'll want to discuss an election date when next we meet."

His face flushed, red creeping up his neck. "Of course."

With that, I parted, not bidding them good day, not acknowledging them further. An unspoken criticism, but not a subtle one. My father would be turning in his grave, I could practically hear his gentle rebuke.

You know better, Kit. Don't let them rattle you.

I strode through the palace, smiling, and nodding at guards and maids, dimly aware of the man and woman at my back. The bodyguards followed me everywhere, silent, and watchful, keeping me safe.

Since my coronation, there'd only been three attempts on my life— each easily handled. Hardly worth the fuss.

I caught sight of my mother's handmaid ahead, calling, "Pauline? Where is my mother?"

The maid dipped her head in greeting,

bobbing up. "In her parlour, Ma'am. Should I bring tea?"

I glanced at my watch and shook my head. "No, I only have a few minutes. Thank you."

She bobbed again, then hurried on her way, no doubt to fulfill some needless endeavour my mother had tasked her with.

These days, my mother preferred solitude but with a house full of staff, that quiet was rare.

I opened the doors to the parlour, finding her exactly where I expected, by the window sitting in the sun, sorting letters. We received hundreds of letters a day, and yet my mother always dealt with them personally, sometimes responding herself, other times asking my siblings. Rarely, but sometimes, she asked me to put pen to paper, and each time I did it knowing it meant as much to her as to the receiver of the missive.

"Darling." Mother gestured me over, tilting her head as she read the tension on my face. "Sit, tell me what's happened."

I wanted to drop and slump, wanted to stamp my foot and pout like a three-year-old. Instead, I settled gracefully, adopting the perfect straight-backed posture that had been drilled into me since birth.

"The men wish me to marry."

Mother pursed her lips but didn't comment.

"It's ridiculous," I told her with a frown. "Isn't it?"

She seemed to weigh her words, glancing at the bodyguards positioned by the door, then back at me.

I swallowed knowing she was about to deliver advice I had no wish to hear.

"Marriage isn't easy, Kit." She reached out, taking my hand in hers. "And marriage to a monarch? To *the* Monarch?" She shook her head. "It is its own kind of torture."

Her lips quirked; her eyes sad. "Your father and I had many wonderful years together before your grandfather passed. But when he took the throne, even then I wasn't prepared for the changes in our life. Oh, your grandmother tried. She advised me well. But as Queen or King, your loyalty isn't to your partner. Your loyalty should and always will be to your people. The crown demands nothing less." She blinked, tears shimmering on her lashes.

"Your father tried. He made time for you, Leo, and Charlotte. He carved out hours to sit with me. But it's not the same as it was. And I found that the partner I married, the man so easy to laugh, retreated behind the weight of his responsibility. And yet it was during this time that he needed me more than he'd ever needed me before."

She squeezed my hand. "Your husband will never know you as anything but Queen. And, my darling, you *do* need to marry. You're the first Queen in the long history of our great nation. Your ascension has been nothing but good news. You're doing wonderful, dear. But you need a partner."

"I need an heir," I corrected her.

"No, darling. You need a *partner*. Someone to share your burdens. Someone who you can lean on when times are tough. The *only* person you can trust. Someone to remind you to have fun, to laugh."

She let go of my hand, rifling through the papers until she pulled a letter from a small stack and handed it over.

The letter was short, general greetings and what-not, but my eyes found and held on the picture, a printed photo of my father and mother. They were at a school, my father watching as my mother attempted to play soccer with the children. They were both young, the photo taken a few years after he'd assumed the mantle of Kingship. His head was thrown back, laughing as he stood in a group of solemn-faced adults while Mother had been caught mid-kick, her skirts hiked up around her knees, surrounded by a tribe of delighted children.

"The advisors hated me that day. Such a lack of decorum." She chuckled, her eyes twinkling. "Your father had been visiting the school and I'd tagged along. He'd been under such pressure to perform, still settling into his role. Everyone expected so much of him— exactly as they do you. They always demanded, never asking what he wanted." She grinned. "I scored the goal and I do believe that was the night we conceived your brother."

"Ew, Mother." I made a face and she laughed, reaching over to tap the letter.

"The son of the photographer sent it. He thought I'd appreciate the memory; I shall be writing to thank him."

Just as I knew she would. I looked down at the paper in my hands, tracing my thumb over my father's face.

"I miss him," I whispered.

"I know. We all do."

I looked up, seeing my mother through new eyes. "You want me to marry."

"I do, my darling. It is my most heartfelt desire."

I blinked, tears burning for some unknown reason. "But why?"

My mother's touch was gentle as she

cupped my face. "Because, my beautiful girl. You may be Queen, but you are still a woman. Rarely do you get your heart's desire. You no longer smile or laugh as freely as you did. You no longer tease or joke. When your father died, it's as if the spark inside you died as well."

"I'm busy. I don't have time for—"

"Hush," my mother ordered, her tone soft steel. "I understand, Kit. But love, true love? It requires a spark. And you have long been tinder waiting to ignite. Once you experience it, nothing will stop you. You'll burn so brightly, my darling. And you deserve it. You deserve to experience that wondrous love. You deserve to feel the flames of passion, to know yourself, and know you are so very, very loved for who you are."

"I don't know where to start," I admitted, finally revealing my deepest fear. "And I'm scared. Terrified, actually. I'll be marrying for life. There is no divorce for me." I swallowed. "What if I make the wrong choice?"

"But what if you make the right one?"

2

———

KATHERINE

Queen's Study, The Royal Palace

I served tea, watching the Prime Minister seated across from me. He looked ill at ease.

"September eighteenth," he finally said, rubbing a hand across his brow. "If that suits, Your Majesty."

I glanced at my secretary who stood by the door. She looked down at the tablet in her hands, quickly swiping fingers across the screen. After a moment she looked up, giving me a short nod.

I'd already known the weekend would be free. I'd kept every Saturday in September clear for the last two years, such was my desire to see this weasel of a man gone.

Impartial, Kit. You must remain impartial.

"I shall ready the banns," I told him, gracefully lifting his cup and saucer and handing it over.

"Ah, about that." The man took the offered tea but set it immediately down on the low table between us. "I was hoping we could postpone for a week or two."

I tilted my head slightly, annoyance twisting in my gut. "But you've named a date, Prime Minister. By the law dissolution of government is to occur later today. The election—"

"Will come," he agreed, interrupting me. He blinked, as if realising his mistake.

"My apologies, it's just...." He reached into his pocket, pulling a handkerchief free and dabbing at his brow. "I'm afraid we have a caucus meeting tonight and...." He trailed off, staring down at the damp cloth in his hand.

"And?" I prompted when he didn't speak.

"I'm about to be overthrown," he admitted, reaching for the tea. He lifted the delicate cup but took no drink, instead staring into the dark liquid as if it held the answer to his future.

"Overthrown? By who?"

"Jonathan Tuhana," he spat the name, making it sound like a curse.

Jonathan's image rose in my mind like an

unwanted demon-- demanding, beautiful, overwhelming.

Young, powerful, and charismatic, the politician was a force to be reckoned with. He wore his heritage proudly, often partaking in the traditional dances and blessings of the Manari people. He'd quickly worked his way up the ranks of the conservative party, endearing himself to young and old, firmly holding a centralist line.

And yet he didn't fit the type. He didn't fall entirely in line with the party ideals. He challenged. He pushed. He called out when he saw injustice being served. He represented a new breed of conservatives, a younger generation who wanted radical change—and was willing to meet the opposition in the middle.

A far cry from the man before me who could barely make it through a meeting without casting aspersions against those across the aisle.

"You should be worried," the Prime Minister told me, finally meeting my gaze. "If he wins, he'll call for a referendum. He hates everything the Monarchy represents."

Does he? Or are you attempting to sway me to your argument, Prime Minister?

I calmly sipped from my cup, considering my next move.

"Has he a good chance?"

The Prime Minister grunted, dropping the delicate cup back into the saucer with a noisy clatter. "He'll be leader by tomorrow."

How interesting.

The palace had eyes and ears everywhere, word should have reached me long before this moment. Instead, this coup must have been silent and swift.

"You'll resign then?"

"Yes." He mopped his brow once more. "Call the election, say it's time for new blood, then hand over to the blackguard."

I ignored the insult. "What does he hold over you?"

The Prime Minister's gaze snapped to mine, his eyes widening a fraction.

"Come, Tony. We both know there's only one reason you'd ever leave the leadership."

He swallowed. "It matters not but that I'm gone."

I allowed him that for I'd find out soon enough.

"Well," I gestured at a maid who stood on the far side of the room. "If this is to be our last meeting then I suspect we should toast to your next endeavour."

We sipped whiskey as we discussed affairs of state and what he would do in his retirement, then a scant thirty minutes later I bid farewell to the pompous jackass.

Not so pompous now.

My secretary, Victoria, hovered nearby.

"Did you know?" I asked, watching Tony's car slowly roll down the long drive, leaving the palace grounds.

For the final time I should hope.

"Not until he confirmed it."

I arched an eyebrow, giving her a look. "But you suspected and didn't tell me?"

She swallowed. "Jonathan, I mean Mr. Tuhana, had been seen in most electorates over the last month." She pulled out her tablet, handing it to me. "But we had no intelligence that this was on the card. We felt it better to wait for confirmation before raising with you."

I flicked through the map, clicking on each of the points to see who he'd met with and when.

"Impressive," I murmured begrudgingly.

Alone, each of these events looked innocent. They were within his portfolio, health and education announcements, visits to projects. But together?

Together, they were a patchwork of masterful manoeuvring. He'd been meeting with core donors, strategic party players, and the old guard to stage this takeover.

"How did Tony not see this?" I muttered, flicking through, then pausing as I landed on one of the event photos.

Jonathan wore traditional dress, his chest bare but for his tribal tattoos, a colourful grass weave skirt hung low on his hips. In his hand he gripped a spear, no doubt one passed through his family line, judging by the faded colours. Around his shoulders hung a *peripuni*, or warrior cape, made from the skins of the giant tufted boar that lived in the mountains to our north. Adorning the cape were the stories of his ancestors told through the bright paint and beads, feathers, and braids that decorated the hide.

I had one similar, passed to me by my mother's mother— the women in my family were fierce warriors, their blood line now that of a queen.

"He's a fine-looking man," Victoria murmured, giving her eyebrows a little wiggle. "And single."

I closed the image, handing the tablet back to her. "And a conservative." I shot her a wry smile. "No matter how attractive a man is, they somehow seem less so when they can't seem to accept the rule of a woman."

Her eyebrows rose in surprise. "That's not it, surely? He seems against the crown, not against you personally."

"It seems that way, doesn't it?"

"Do you know him?"

I swallowed, closing my eyes for a brief moment. "Long ago I did. Now? No. We've not spoken in years."

"And? Thoughts?"

I shrugged. "Who he is now is vastly different to who he was then." I gestured around the space with a wave of my hand. "But then, we all changed."

"Do you worry he won't fall into line?"

I paused, considering her words. "No. I worry he'll seek to challenge me in the same way he did Tony. And an insurrection is never a welcome prospect."

Victoria swallowed audibly. "What will you do if he wins?"

My lips quirked. "What I do best. Reign."

3

KATHERINE

Parliament House

Parliament House had fast become one of my least favourite places to visit. But as Monarch it was my duty to attend every sitting of parliament.

With the government dissolved due to the election, my duty now didn't involve sitting while listening to adults sling insults at each other over the cost of potatoes. Today, my duty was to call the banns for the election, and listen as the political parties put forward their leaders for my acceptance.

While there were two main political parties in Astipia, we had numerous minorities— all of which, tradition dictated, I bless.

The limo glided to a halt at the front of the

building, my personal bodyguards getting out to shift the paparazzi back.

"How do I look?" I asked Victoria, pulling at the *peripuni* that was draped across my shoulders.

"Like a queen."

I rolled my eyes, letting out a small huffing laugh. "Well played."

She chuckled, then the door opened and my mask dropped once more.

I slipped from the vehicle, a smile painted on my face.

Questions were hurled my way as I began the long walk into the building.

"Your Majesty! What do you think of Jonathan Tuhana?"

"Your Majesty! Mr. Tuhana is an open conservative! Do you have any comments on his position?"

The news had broken early this morning. Tony Privatey was out, Jonathan Tuhana was in. The caucus didn't normally release voting numbers, but someone had leaked it to the press. He'd won by an overwhelming majority.

Tony was a fool if he hadn't seen it coming.

I made my way through the crowd and up to the entry, the herald waiting for me.

"Your Majesty." He bowed, then gestured

for me to lead. "The throne room is ready to receive you."

I walked the familiar path, my footsteps gentle on the cobblestone flooring. These were the same floors my ancestors had walked, conducting this very duty.

History always repeats.

At the door, the herald lifted his drum, beating out the quick rhythm that had become the soundtrack to my life. A hush descended as the herald announced me to the packed throne room. With a smile at him, I made my way down the gentle sloped walkway to the throne.

Throughout the centuries our tribal practices had remained a tried and true guide, a link back to country and spirit. The design of this room reflected one such practice.

In the Manari culture, no chief or king sat above the people they served. Back before we'd built stone cities, our villages had been shaped like amphitheatres, the chief's tent at the centre but below all those around it.

When the King had decided to build the original city, the first woman of my line had convinced her new husband to adopt the same practice, explaining that it would guide his acceptance with the tribes. And so it was. When the labourers had built our parliament and castles, laying the stone foundations for our most important places, they had done so using the design of the Manari. These buildings had no stairs, and contained no elevated stages. Instead, everyone could enter our parliament, all were equal, except the monarch who sat below them, a reminder that it was their leader's responsibility to lift them up, and a reminder for the leader of the weight that sat upon their shoulders.

And so it would always be.

I took my place before my throne, looking up at the gathered, taking a moment to smooth my *peripuni* and settle myself before speaking.

"We gather here today on the lands of my ancestors." I pulled dirt from the pouch at my waist, throwing it in an arc before me. "Under the sky of our Gods." I tossed the rest of the dirt up in an arch over my head.

I began to walk around the dais. "I welcome you to the lands of my people." I began reciting the *welcome to country* in the language of my people.

"Ma ninj unka murandjeri ualluk yeara ualluk mena knoodei maik."

We are part of this land and the land is part of us.

"Ullabinj whalin ulumni ma compeitie. Uenuar whalin mar tuum dius."

This is where we come from. This is where our spirits return.

"Ma uenuar Manari ualluk boodgas mar ullniak. Mar hueori ullauk une quorum anu sacis. Farun la nori boodgas burgu. Han la for toogi ualluk, fori for toogi la. Boodgas."

We, the people of this land, welcome you to our country. Our traditional lands are ancient and sacred. May you be welcome with respect. If you look after the land, it will look after you. Welcome.

The words were as old as time, engraved into my soul. They were the first words a child heard upon their birth, and the last they would hear before being lowered into the ground.

It was our blessing and reminder of the land on which we lived.

The herald struck up a beat, the tattoo pounding through my chest, hard and fierce.

In time to the beat, I scooped more dirt from my pouch, throwing it across the cobblestone floor in practiced movements.

From east to west, from north to south, from sky to sea and mountain to plain, you represent the best of us, Kit. When you welcome people to our lands you do so on behalf of me, of your mother, of your grandmother and your warrior ancestors. You represent our tribe, Kit. Our legacy. You are a moment in time, the person

*who is a culmination of all who came before
you, and the beginning of all who come after.
You, my daughter, are alive.*

My father's voice always came to me in
moments like this, when the world faded and
movement overtook me, guiding each sweep of
my hand, each tap of my foot, each dip of my
shoulder or tip of my head.

With a final quick beat, the drum fell silent
and I slapped my hands on the ground sending
dust flying.

Applause burst over me, taking away from
the moment. I pushed to my feet, pressing my
hands to my heart space, bowing my head.

"Patricia Abigail," my aide called, inviting
the first applicant to step forward.

The woman, an independent, stepped close
waiting. I reached for her, pulling her clasped
hand to my chest, pressing my forehead to hers.

"Boodgas," I greeted. "Uhra im gagado fa
mar."

Welcome. May the Gods be with you.

With that my blessing was complete and
Patricia stepped back, curtseying low. "And
with you, my Queen."

On and on it went, one candidate after
another, all of them receiving my blessing.

"Jonathan Tuhana," my aide called, my
body stiffening in response.

Jonathan stepped forward, his own *peripuni* covering his broad shoulders. Underneath, he wore a tailored navy-blue suit. When paired with his *peripuni* it somehow made him seem less civilized, as if he were a wolf in sheep's clothing.

A shiver ran down my spine as I met his green gaze, the colour just as stunning as I remembered. They held a question in their depths that I had no way of answering.

My pulse beat in my neck as he stepped closer holding out his large hand for me to clasp.

He's just a man, Kit. Just another candidate to greet and bless.

I linked our fingers, noting the rough skin of his palm, the calluses on his fingertips.

This is no mere politician.

In a practiced move, I pulled his arm to my chest, lifting my head slightly to press our foreheads together.

"Boodgas. Uhra im gagado fa mar," I told him, the words coming out breathy and soft as I tried to ignore the heat of his arm on my breast, a contrast to the silky cool of his hair as it brushed against my forehead.

He squeezed my fingers, his skin warm against mine, his fingers inadvertently brushing my breast.

I moved to let go but he held me for a moment longer, his gaze raking my face.

"Jus uhra ehra hamn mar, il Giisera."

And may they be with you, my Queen.

With that he allowed me to let go, stepping back to fall to one knee, bowing in the manner of our warrior ancestors.

Around us, cameras snapped capturing the moment a warrior honoured his Queen.

A warrior who may soon rule.

My aide called the next name and I looked away, pasting a smile I didn't feel on my lips.

You'd do well to stay away from Jonathan Tuhana.

The hairs on the back of my neck prickled and I shifted, catching sight of Jonathan as he rose. Our eyes met, his filled with hunger and heated desire.

For a moment I held his gaze, glorying in the spark that flamed between us. Then, with deliberation, I broke eye contact, welcoming the next candidate, determined to hide how rattled he had left me.

He's dangerous.

To my heart or my people?

That is yet to be determined.

4

———

JONATHAN

The Great Hall, Parliament House

I sipped the rich wine, allowing the chatter around me to flow. As was tradition, all candidates were required to attend a dinner following the ceremony. We would feast and be merry tonight, only to resume our cutthroat brand of politics tomorrow.

I caught sight of a flash of feathers, my gaze pulled from the candidates on either side of me, to the head table where the Queen presided.

Katherine was a handsome woman, though not beautiful in any traditional sense. She was far too aloof to be considered friendly, too regal to be considered merely pretty, and too stern to be considered beautiful.

But being in her presence felt electric. She

shone. Glowed. The candidates rotated in and out from her table between each course, and she welcomed them all with ready smiles and open ears. It took no more than three, perhaps four minutes for laughter to be expressed, and smiles to turn from courteous to adoring.

She had a way about her that compelled adulation, and I found that I was not immune.

My advisor and best friend leaned in toward me, turning his head slightly to murmur in my ear.

"Don't fuck this up."

I chuckled, picking up my wine and taking a long sip, considering him over the delicate glass. "Where is your faith, Patrick?"

He rolled his eyes before shrewdly considering the room. "We've been working towards this moment for ten years. We can't afford for you to cock it up at the final moment."

"And somehow, despite your overwhelming lack of confidence in my abilities, here we are." I gestured to the room at large. "Perhaps even you can admit I did good."

"Don't be an idiot, of course you've performed well." He shifted, straightening his suit jacket. "But this is just the start, Jon. The change you want requires sacrifices the likes of which you can't even imagine."

Oh, I can imagine.

It had been all I'd thought about for the last ten years as I sacrificed my morals and soul to get to this very moment.

Winning the election will make it all worth it.

Laughter from the Queen's table drew my attention. The Queen's smile met her eyes for perhaps the first time all evening.

A thread of desire worked its way through me, anticipation coiling.

The election will make it all worth it.... Or will she?

"You can't manipulate that one," Patrick commented quietly. "She's out of your league."

I cleared my throat, forcing my gaze away from our country's most dazzling jewel. "I don't plan on manipulating her."

He snorted into his wine glass.

I plan on marrying her.

5

———————

KATHERINE

The Great Hall, Parliament House

I tried not to be distracted by the man across the room. Dinners like this could be tedious affairs filled with meaningless chit-chat and monotonous observations. I'd often find myself with a barnacle or two, the individuals in question clinging desperately to me as if I were where they would find salvation or meaning.

I am nothing but a face for a crown. A body that must become a vessel for the next generation.

Awareness simmered in my blood, the faint vibration of attraction licking at my skin as I made small talk with yet another table of candidates.

The waiters began to clear away the penultimate course, the signal for those seated at the table that it was to move on.

"Thank you so much for your time, Your Majesty," the older woman gushed enthusiastically. "I'll be sure to count on your vote at the election."

"I'm afraid I'm unable to vote, Ms. Green. It would be against the constitution for me to participate in something in which I must, rightly, remain impartial."

"Of course." She gave me a wink. "Impartial from your crown all the way to your wee little toes."

On the inside I bristled, frustrated by both her tone and condescension.

Do not question my loyalty or integrity, madam. In years gone by I'd have had your head.

The words, like so many others, burned like acid on the tip of my tongue, begging to be set free. And they, like every other, were swallowed back down, left to simmer and corrode in my belly.

"Your Majesty." The warm greeting elicited a primal response in me, desire heating my blood, my body clenching as I twisted, taking him in.

I noted with approval that he still wore his

peripuni, the feathers fluttering gently as he bowed, waiting for me to grant permission for him to approach.

"Mr. Tuhana, please, take a seat."

Behind him the rest of the table began to follow, each curtseying or bowing until they had all been invited to sit.

I glanced at the clock on the far side of the dining room, mentally tallying the length of time it would take before I could escape. A headache had begun to build behind my right eye, a sure indication that I'd been exposed to far too much flash photography.

"Your Majesty? Coffee? Tea?" The senior waiter hovered at my elbow.

"Tea, peppermint if you have it. Also, if you could assist, I'd love if you could ask my assistant to call Thompson about the fountain. I quite forgot to do it today and it needs to happen tonight. She'll know what I'm asking for."

"Of course!" The waiter bowed, obviously thrilled to be of assistance. I wouldn't burst his bubble by telling him there was no fountain, the direction was a cleverly veiled code that indicated I needed some ibuprofen, quickly.

Experienced waiters refilled glasses and took coffee or tea orders then slipped away, leaving me with the final candidates.

I looked around the table taking stock of each of the faces before me. Conservatives and progressives were purposefully intermingled, a ploy on my behalf in an attempt to encourage bipartisanship. My biggest fear remained polarization of ideals, that our political system would become so corroded, so infested with personality and ego rather than integrity and community that we disintegrated into infighting.

Not on my watch.

I raised my wine glass, which had been filled throughout the night with sparkling water, offering the table a welcoming smile. "To the election. May the Gods be with you as you serve our people."

"And you," the table echoed, glasses clinking.

While we all drank, I considered the table, weighing who would be the best to engage first, who would guide the others to interact, who would be a problem, who I'd need to encourage.

A lifetime of training had gifted me with the ability to assess people with one glance. Rarely did they surprise me these days, and yet here I sat, surprised when it was not Mr. Tuhana who started the conversation but the meek Ms. Laney Hazelwood, an Independent.

"My Queen, you sent two bills back for debate—a virtually unheard of event. Do you expect to do the same with the new government?"

I caught sight of Victoria making her way to our table, moving in time to intersect the waiter carrying our dishes. In a practiced move she'd slip my pain medication onto the plate so when I lifted them to my lips no one would be the wiser.

A queen must never show weakness. That particular lesson had been drilled into me following my father's funeral. Where my father had been praised for his vulnerability, I was scorned.

A woman cannot show emotion.

"A good question, Ms. Hazelwood. But one I'm afraid I can't answer. The circumstances of those two bills have little bearing on those brought to me in the future. I consider each on its own merit. But if you are asking will I continue this practice of returning them to the parliament, then the answer is yes. Every motion, every bill, every decision must be weighed against the good of the people. If I am not persuaded that it is the best option then I will return it for further work."

"Doesn't that overstep the role of

monarch?" Ms. Hazelwood's companion asked, his expression dark and judging.

What the devil is his name? George? Geoff? Jim? Something like that. Either way, I don't like him.

"I quite think the role of the monarch is to unify. Unlike our British cousins, I'm honour bound to interject in the political sphere when the needs of the people aren't being met. Rarely has that been the case, but the recent introductions and overwhelming objection from the populace issued in the form of protests guided my decisions."

The man's lips twisted into a thin line and something glinted in his eye.

The waiter placed my dessert in front of me, the pills strategically hidden in the form of a dinner mint that had been added to the plate.

Gods bless, Victoria.

"Please," I reached for my spoon. "Let's eat."

I spooned a mouthful of the rich panna cotta, savouring the taste for a moment as the table began to eat. Temporarily distracted by their meal, I unwrapped my pain medication, quickly slipping it into my mouth and taking a sip of the sparkling water to down them.

They'd kick in quickly and I'd be able to get

through the rest of tonight, and perhaps, sleep later.

I turned to the woman seated on my left, opening my mouth to ask after her son when Jim-Geoff-George interrupted, calling my attention back.

"You say you're guided by the protests, but what happens if you ignore them?"

I suppressed a frustrated sigh, ignoring the tickle of annoyance at his question.

"I believe that would be to my detriment. Many a leader has ignored the calls of their people only to find themselves no longer in a leadership position." I smiled, attempting to close the conversation. "Thankfully, I'd say our country is rational enough to settle our differences by words rather than violence."

I twisted, turning to Mrs. Helen Johnson. "Now, Mrs. Johnson, you must tell me how your son is doing. I hear he's attending Oxford now?"

"Death to the Monarch!"

From the corner of my eye, Geoff-Jim-George pulled a knife from his jacket, shoving up from the table.

Oh, fuck.

My training kicked in. Already in motion, I rocked back on my chair, tipping it over. I tucked my head then rolled backward, cartwheeling until my feet hit the ground, allowing me to spring up, arms at the defensive.

The man advanced, the knife waving wildly as diners scrambled and my bodyguards fought through the crowd, struggling to get to my side.

They're not going to make it.

The knife-wielding extremist was far too close.

Focus, Kit. Today is not your day to die.

He advanced one step, then another, leaping towards me with a swing. I dipped, the knife slicing through the air where my body had just been.

Look for a weakness, keep out of reach, stay alive until the guards arrive.

I pulled back as he made to swing again. Just as he drew his arm back, an almighty roar echoed through the room and a blur of movement distracted him. Jonathan, his head dropped and shoulders braced, charged at the knife-wielding lunatic.

The extremist whirled, attempting to scare Jonathan off with his knife but he was far too late. Jonathan caught him around the waist, lifting him into the air, then slamming him down in a full body crash. The knife skittered across the floor, and I dove, scrambling to snatch it before the man could do further damage.

Jonathan reared back, his fist pounding into the man's face, his expression fierce as blood splattered, dotting clothes, table cloths and skin.

And I thought a headache was the worst part of this day.

Bodyguards arrived a moment later, pulling Jonathan from the man, as others pinned Geoff-Jim-George, shoving his bleeding face to the floor and handcuffing him as he continued to call for my death.

A single thought penetrated the shock surrounding me.

If he'd succeeded, I'd have been the first heirless monarch to die in over three hundred years.

I swallowed, turning away from the arrest, straightening my clothing, and patting my hair.

No weakness. No weakness. You may break later, Kit. Now you need to be Queen.

With a deep breath I yanked on my emotions, forcing them into a box and locking it tight.

Today I must be less than a woman and more than a queen. I must be warrior and justice, vengeance and peace. I must be all equally if I'm to prevent this from escalating.

"Your Majesty, are you hurt?"

The gentle voice had me turning, a smile painted on my face.

"I'm fine, Victoria. Thank you." I threw back my shoulders, my *peripuni* sliding back slightly, settling into place. "Good. Then let's check on the guests. I imagine the police will be here shortly, no doubt the media following hot on their heels. I don't want any misinformation spread about my welfare."

She nodded, her face pale behind her large glasses. "Of course. They're moving them into side rooms. They all need to be interviewed, statements taken and what-not before they can leave."

"Are you alright?" I asked, reaching over to brush a stray petal from her lapel.

She nodded, then shook her head, then nodded again. "Yes, I mean, no. But yes. He saved you. Jonathan. He looked like... like...."

Like a warrior.

"Come, Victoria," I swept past her, straightening my shoulders, and lifting my head, determined to present a picture of health and calm. "Let's see to our guests."

6

JONATHAN

The Great Hall, Parliament House

Hours had passed since the attack but still adrenaline surged through my veins, my body alert to any potential attack.

As a young man I'd been a soldier, serving my country in wars created by men I'd never met. I'd lost friends; brothers, and sisters whose blood I still carried on my skin.

"Well, if that doesn't win you the election, I don't know what will," Patrick remarked, leaning against the wall beside me.

I shot him a side glance, then turned back to watch the guests as they mingled. For the majority, the adrenaline had worn off. Between the police taking statements, the waitstaff handing out drinks, food and blankets, and the Queen making sure she spoke to each and every attendee, they'd begun to process the shock.

"The first exclusive interview with a guest has finally hit the news," Patrick remarked, playing with his phone. "They must have started releasing the guests." He laughed, still scrolling through his phone. "The Queen issued a formal statement immediately after the incident and another just now. Do you think they have that kind of thing pre-prepared?"

I ignored him, my gaze on the woman standing with a group of teary-eyed strangers offering them comfort.

"You're playing well in the media. They're calling you a hero. We can use this. I'm seeing an ad campaign around—"

"Patrick?"

"Mm?"

"Shut the fuck up."

His mouth snapped close, his head bowing as he continued to scroll through his news feed.

The Queen produced tissues, handing them to a distraught woman and offering her a gentle hug.

"Oh, that's a good shot."

I turned, seeing Patrick snap a photo of the moment.

"Patrick!"

"Nope." He held up a finger, shaking it at me. "You employed me to be your campaign manager. I'm doing what I do best—campaigning. Don't shoot me for being the political powerhouse that will win you that coveted position."

I ground my teeth together, too full of fire and fury to remain near him a moment longer.

"I'll be in the garden. Call if they want me."

I craved the freedom of sky and stars, cold air on my face and the earth under my feet, needing the connection to the land to rid me of this terrible raging fear.

Outside I found silence and stillness, yet was still unable to find my calm.

He tried to kill her. To slit her throat. He wanted blood and destruction and not one person stood between them. If she hadn't rolled....

The door on the far side of the garden opened, a woman stepping out into the cool air.

My Queen.

"Please," Katherine said, holding a hand out to halt someone behind her. "I just need a moment."

"We need to clear the garden, ma'am."

She sighed. "If I stay within arm's distance of the door, will you allow me a moment? The only way to get into the garden would be through this door or via grappling hooks from above. You've already swept it once. Please, Alec. I need a moment."

I stepped forward, clearing my throat, Alec immediately palmed his gun, his hand sweeping Katherine back behind him.

"I'm the only one here," I said with a shrug. "If Your Majesty doesn't mind the company, I wouldn't be opposed to remaining out here for a few moments more."

Alec considered me; his face impassive. "You're the one who wrestled the radical."

My lips twisted into a half smile. "Yeah. Learned that one in Turkey."

Alec relaxed, glancing around the garden. "You sure you're alone?"

"Yep."

"Ma'am?"

Katherine eyed me, her expression blank. After a long moment she turned to Alec.

"I'll be fine. Stay close. I just need a few minutes of fresh air."

He nodded, sent a meaningful glance my way, then moved back inside, shutting the door.

"Mr. Tuhana?"

"Yes, my Queen?"

"Will you turn around please? I understand you need to look after me but I want a moment alone."

I nodded, turning slowly even though I was loathed to do so.

In the quiet of the night I heard her move, her feet light as she shifted through the space, then settled, falling silent.

For a long moment we neither moved nor spoke, the only sounds coming from the road on the far side of the building, and the soft sounds that accompanied the night.

"I owe you a debt, Mr. Tuhana."

"Jonathan," I corrected, keeping my back to her. "Please. Or Jon."

She paused, as if surprised by my request.

"Alright. I owe you a debt, Jon. And while a Prime Ministership is beyond even my capability to give you, I'd like to offer you a favour. You need only say what you wish and if it is within my power then I'll try to grant it."

My heart hammered through my chest, the pounding reminded me of the drums my ancestors used to signal war.

"May I approach?"

"Yes."

I pivoted on my heel, closing the few lengths to her.

She sat on a stone bench, her spine curved, her expression tired and guarded.

"I have only one wish, my Queen."

Something passed over her face, something fearful yet excited.

"Speak, warrior."

I leaned in, bending until my mouth sat parallel to her ear, ensuring that she would hear every word I uttered.

"As the warrior who saved your life, I ask for the right to invoke the *akaternok ah yalonel.*"

She sucked in a breath, pulling away from me, surging to her feet.

"You can't! You're to be Prime Minister. You're unable to be both."

I stepped forward, closing the gap between us. "For you? I'd resign. If you accept my right then I'll do it, I'll step away. I'll fall into line. I'll do whatever you bid."

Her gaze raked my face. "But why?"

I suppressed a smile, shifting back as I heard the door behind us open. "Accept and I'll tell you."

Her assistant called to her from the doorway. "My Queen, the police are ready for you."

She stared at me for a moment longer, then turned, brushing past me.

"Speak to Victoria, she'll organise a private dinner for later this week. We'll discuss your request then."

And with that, she was gone, disappearing into the building leaving only the subtle scent of peach on the air.

KATHERINE

Queen's Bedchamber, The Royal Palace

I lay awake, staring at the ceiling, the pain in my temples refusing to subside as I replayed Jon's words over and over.

As the warrior who saved your life, I ask for the right to invoke the akaternok ah yalonel.

Akaternok ah yalonel, the marriage claim.

A tradition of my ancestors, I'd not heard of it being used for centuries, not since the tribes had merged during the industrial revolution, or, perhaps, even earlier.

I ask for the right to invoke the akaternok ah yalonel.

I groaned, turning on my side, scrunching

my eyes shut as I tried to banish both Jon and the headache from my mind.

A claim of *akaternok ah yalonel* could only be granted if it met three criteria. First, the man or woman had to have rescued that person from a life-or-death situation. Second, the warrior wanted to invoke *akaternok ah yalonel* to offer a lifetime of protection. The final condition was that the rescued party had to agree.

The *akaternok ah yalonel* didn't include a provision for love. It didn't force me to honour and obey. It didn't ask anything but for me to be committed to the person who had saved my life for the rest of my days.

And for them to do the same.

As the warrior who saved your life....

As Monarch I couldn't just meet those three criteria and be done with it. I needed to consider if he would be the best candidate for Prince Consort. If he would work with me for the good of my people.

I closed my eyes, pinching the bridge of my nose in the dark, considering all I knew of Jonathan.

A lifetime ago, we'd been children who played together while our mothers lunched. Not because we dwelled in the same spheres of influence, but because my mother had championed Mallory House, the charity his mother had founded.

As we grew older, those playdates had changed in tone, and for a while I'd nursed a small crush on Jonathan. Then his mother had passed away and he'd enrolled to serve in our military forces, and life had moved on.

It had been many years since we'd seen each other, and many more since we'd had any form of meaningful conversation.

He'd have to resign. He'd be forced into an untenable position, and so would you. This could be seen as favouritism or worse— collusion. And he's a conservative. Is that what you want, Kit? To be tied to a man whose own party brings forward bills you're forced to send down?

I didn't have any answers.

I have to marry— now more than ever. The danger is so very real, and my siblings? I wouldn't wish this responsibility upon them.

My child would be groomed as the future Monarch from birth, unlike my siblings who had neither the temperament nor the interest in ruling. Their education had drastically deviated from my own. They'd been free to attend parties and sneak out with few repercussions. It would have been a cold day in hell before those same freedoms would have been allowed for me.

His proposal solves many issues. It balances the conservative and progressives, shows that common ground can be achieved. It's a romantic story that would play well in the press and will likely increase tourism in the lead up to the wedding. He's a citizen and a known and respected entity, few could deny that, particularly after tonight.

And he can give you a child.

I swallowed, a new pain blooming in my chest, distracting me from my headache.

If you say yes there'll have to be terms. A contract will need to be drawn up that makes it clear what the expectations of his office shall be. He'll be Prince Consort. Your Prince Consort. He'll be offered riches and opportunities all in an effort to gain access to me. Clear guidelines, clear expectations. It's the only way this will work.

And a baby. At least two. An heir and a spare, as is my duty.

I wanted to distance myself from my future children. I wanted to consider them as nothing but names in what would be a long lineage of future royalty.

But I could not. My heart ached for these future babies. They would be the love I would never find. I wanted to shelter and protect them. Adore them. Love them more than my heart could know.

So, it's settled. Victoria can organise for the lawyers to draw up the contract. If Mr. Tuhana agrees, then we shall be married before the election. That will allow time for a small honeymoon prior to the swearing in of the new Prime Minister. We'll be married in the Murmuranay on whatever weekend is available. There will be a public holiday, as is tradition, and we shall retire to the summer house at Kilgarie for our honeymoon.

I nodded as if it were decided. As if I had any say in the matter. As if it were a decision about brunch rather than the rest of my life.

My hand absently rubbed at the skin above the ache in my chest.

I'll talk to Victoria tomorrow. All will be settled when I next meet with Mr. Tuhana.

I closed my eyes determined to fall asleep and ignore the deep well of sadness radiating from where my heart used to be.

8

KATHERINE

Morning Room, The Royal Palace

I lifted the tea cup to my lips to take a sip of the smooth brew. Around the breakfast table sat my mother, my siblings, Victoria, and the head of Palace security.

"And you're sure he was a lone actor?" My brother pressed for the fourth time in as many minutes.

"We cannot rule out the possibility of him being a part of a larger organisation, but at the moment we have no intelligence to tell us otherwise, Your Highness."

"Leo, stop." My mother sighed in exasperation. "The poor man has answered your questions. Tim has nothing more to add. Am I right?" she asked.

Tim nodded. "I'm sorry. I wish I had more but until the intelligence agencies complete their assessment I can't offer anything further."

Mother reached across the table, patting Tim's hand. "That's quite alright, Timothy. We appreciate all your efforts."

Charlotte shook her head. "I just don't understand how he slipped through. Surely the background check would have picked this up."

"It appears we were misled about his attendance. He used his cousin's name, the two being remarkably similar in appearance. The cousin lives in New York and is horrified by this incident."

"And the knife? How did he get that through?"

"We're still investigation. Tim cleared his throat, shifting uncomfortably on his chair. "If there's nothing else then I'll be going."

"Thank you, Tim. That will be—"

I interrupted my mother.

"Just one thing, actually." I set my tea cup in the saucer with a small click, then settled my hands in my lap, forcing calm and reassurance into my voice. "I should like to discuss a particularly sensitive matter that cannot leave this room."

The room immediately cleared of the two bodyguards and one waiter who'd stood off to the side, they knew the process for this sort of request.

I waited for the door to shut before focussing on Tim. "I have decided to marry."

My brother stuttered, choking on a mouthful of coffee. Charlotte dropped her spoon, her mouth agape as she stared at me.

Victoria immediately opened her notebook, pulling a pen from the messy bun on her head and holding it at the ready as she watched me.

Good woman.

Tim and my mother showed zero reaction.

"And who is this man?" Mother asked, reaching for the salt.

"Mr. Tuhana, actually. Following last night's incident, he offered *akaternok ah yalonel*. Pending an extensive background check, risk assessment, and a signed contract outlining his role and the responsibilities that come with being Prince Consort, I expect us to be married before the election."

Silence dominated the table. I persevered.

"Victoria, can you please organise a private meeting with Mr. Tuhana for tomorrow evening. I'd also like a contract drawn up, a prenuptial arrangement. It should also outline the expectations of his station."

She nodded, rapidly taking notes.

I turned to our head of security. "Tim, will

that give you sufficient time to get the necessary screening checks completed? I should like to know if there are any skeletons in the closet, I should be aware of."

Tim nodded, his face flushing. "I'll do it myself, Your Majesty."

I nodded. "Thank you. Your discretion is appreciated."

"Victoria, Tim? Could you please give us the room?" Mother asked, her dark eyes focussed on me.

"Of course."

They both stood, bowing, then took their leave, hurrying from the room and leaving me with just my family.

Strong heart, Kit. Do not back down from this decision.

"What are you thinking?" Leo exploded, slapping a hand on the table. "Jonathan Tuhana? The man's a conservative! Worse, he's a fucking politician!"

I reached for my cup, waiting for them to get over their excitement.

"Do you love him, Kit?" Charlotte asked, reaching out to touch my arm. "I mean, you knew each other years ago. Have you reconnected?"

For a moment I wanted to lie to her.

"No," I admitted. "I'm sorry, Lottie."

"Is it love at first sight then?"

I shook my head. "You know I'm not built that way. And it's quite hard for me to love someone I hardly know. But he offered and I accepted. He seems like a good man. I expect that love will come with time."

A memory flashed, capturing my attention for a moment. Jonathan rearing back to punch the attacker, his giant bicep pulled back, his body strong and hard.

A little sparkle of desire shimmied down my body to pool deep in my abdomen. My thighs clenched together, my body tightening in response.

Lust and love are not mutually exclusive.

"Have you told anyone?" Leo asked urgently. "Anyone besides those in this room?"

"No, but don't try to talk me out of it, Leo. I've made my decision and I'm quite determined to see it through—pending any outcomes of the background check of course."

"Of course," echoed Mother, her eyebrows raised in amusement. "I should have known you'd go about this marriage business in much the same way as you do everything— efficiently and without grand circumstance."

Charlotte rolled her eyes. "Grand circumstance? Really, Mother?"

"You're the one who fell in love with a

prince in a week in Morocco. Where is Frederick, by the way?" Leo asked.

"At his summer house, if you must know." Charlotte sniffed, glaring at him. "He's wining and dining some exporters."

Leo snorted. "Is that what they call it?"

"Do you have a problem with my fiancé?"

"Yeah, I do actually. He's nothing but a goddamned—"

"Children!" Mother snapped. "This is about Kit. Focus!" She twisted back to look at me. "Will you be happy, my darling?"

I paused, considering my answer. "I will," I said, swallowing a lump in my throat. "I may not have the love you and Father enjoyed, but I'll have a peaceful kingdom, a man who will be a sufficient prince consort, children, and you all."

I looked around the table, taking in my family – my sister's watery eyes, my brother's mutinous face, and Mother's calm acceptance.

"I know you all wished more for me but this is what I must do. I love you, and I have no doubts about this direction."

"I don't think you should be making rash decisions following a shock," Leo said, crossing his arms.

"And yet, if I had died you would be King. Are you ready for that, Leo?"

His face paled but his resolve hardened—I could tell by the stubborn set of his jaw.

"I'd do my duty."

"As must I."

This is my cross to bear, and bear it I will.

I pushed back from the table, smoothing hands down my thighs as I stood. "As wonderful as this has been, I'm afraid duty calls."

Mother rose, crossing to press a kiss to my cheek and offer a hug.

"I trust your judgement. But darling, just remember, no one is forcing you to choose between your heart and your head."

"The parliament may. The constitution demands I declare an heir." I pulled back, dipping to collect my phone from the table. "And after last night I expect they'll be calling for my nomination."

She watched me closely. "I knew his mother, Kit. I'm not sure if you remember that."

"I do."

She nodded, a strange expression crossing her face. "His mother spoke about him highly before her death. From all I have heard, he's a good man."

"I expect he is."

Leo slung an arm around me. "This conversation isn't over."

I elbowed him, chuckling when he doubled over. "Yes, it is. Now I really do need to go."

They called goodbye, sitting down at the table to finish their breakfast. For a moment I wanted to stay, joining them for a chat and linger over coffee.

The urge to ditch my duties was strong, nearly overpowering.

You are Queen, Kit. You don't have that option.

I suppressed a sigh, straightened my shoulders. "And Mother?"

"Yes, darling?"

I grinned, throwing her a wink.

"I give you permission to plan the entire event."

She smiled, her eyes twinkling. "Then I expect Victoria and I shall have a rather busy day ahead."

9

JONATHAN

National Arboretum, Sommerland Park

"Ah, it appears the Queen has arrived." Patrick threw me a side-eye. "Were we expecting her after last night?"

I watched Katherine enter the room, noting with approval, and no small amount of relief, her additional guards.

"I expected it. And if you didn't then, honestly, I'd question your political prowess, Pat. She's going to want to send a message after last night. The attack won't derail her."

"Strength and might. I can get behind that."

No. Resilience and fortitude. Perseverance and responsibility.

While I'd not doubted her commitment to presenting a 'business as usual' face, I had to admit surprise at her appearance.

Except for a slight darkening under her eyes, the Queen looked no different than any other day.

"A consummate professional," Patrick sighed, admiration clear in his voice. "Do you think she'd ever renounce the throne and consider a run for the Prime Ministership?"

I snorted, shifting to give him my driest stare. "Never. But it's nice to know where your loyalties lie."

He grinned, slapping me on the shoulder. "Unlike some men, I'm not encumbered by such meaningless trivialities as loyalty and mateship. You and I are of the same ilk. We're out to win."

I glanced back at Katherine, my body tightening as the crowd around her began to grow.

"Perhaps winning isn't all it's cracked up to be."

Patrick started, choking on air. I slapped his back, perhaps slightly harder than I should.

"Not all it's... Jonathan! What the fuck are you saying? This is all you've wanted for years."

I lifted one shoulder in a dismissive gesture. "Perhaps last night changed my priorities."

"More like you have a concussion and none of us realised. I'm calling the doctor. We can't leave this to chance."

I waved him off, focussing on our Queen.

My Queen.

She made her way gracefully around the room, ensuring each of the attendees got a slice of her time.

This is what she does. This is what you will have to reconcile.

Her days would forever be the people's.

But her nights?

Mine. All mine.

I wanted to kiss her brow, soothe the tension I saw hiding there. I wanted to brush the stray hair from her cheek even as I guarded her back, providing another layer of protection.

As if sensing my thoughts, Katherine raised her head, her eyes meeting mine across the room. For a moment our gaze held, and I saw something I hadn't ever expected— desire.

Then the moment was gone, disappearing behind the collegial mask of meaningless banality that she wore.

Lust flared, my body humming, my cock thickening as primal triumph fired my blood. A near overwhelming desire burning in me to walk across the floor and claim my Queen.

"Patrick?"

"Mm?"

"Call a caucus meeting for tonight. I have something I need to do immediately."

He frowned. "What's that?"

I turned away, striding for the door, the priorities of my day shifting. "Resign."

JONATHAN

Private Dining Room, The Royal Palace

The woman across the table considered me over her wine glass. She'd greeted me with the same ready warmth that she offered to every person she met, but I wanted more.

I want lust and love. I want desire and flushed cheeks. I want glassy eyes and panting breaths. I want her under me. I want her nights and her days.

I want her heart.

My cock pressed against the fly of my slacks, hard and insistent. It'd been so since the moment I'd walked in the room.

My Queen had dressed for seduction.

She rarely wore her hair down in public, but tonight her long locks flowed like silky midnight water down her shoulders, and over her breasts and back. She'd occasionally brush a stray lock away from her face, the ends trailing along the swells of her breasts before being discarded.

Yet another thing she rarely revealed in public. In fact, while most of her outfits were dresses or nicely pressed slacks and tailored blouses, the Queen rarely revealed her figure—often being compared to a primly dressed school marm. Rare were the times she showed any decolletage, and, casting my mind back, I could only think of evening events where ballgowns were paired with her *peripuni*.

"Kari?"

The guard started, the sole occupant of the room beside ourselves.

"Majesty?"

"Could you give us the room please?"

She hesitated, then nodded. "Of course. I'll be outside, call if you need me."

We both waited, the Queen sipping her wine while the bodyguard exited.

As the door clicked shut, Katherine raised her head, considering me with those deep, dark eyes.

She is stunning.

Anticipation hummed through my veins, my blood buzzing under my skin. I'd been waiting all night for her to address my proposal and had a feeling this would be the moment.

"I must admit, I was surprised to learn that you've resigned."

I started, my eyebrows lifting. "You know about that?"

A small smile teased at the edge of her lips. "A queen knows all, Jonathan."

"Jon," I corrected absently. "Have I made the right choice? My caucus thinks not. They've given me twenty-four hours to come to my senses."

"That's because the polls have swung to eighty-three percent in your favour. Should they go to the ballot box tomorrow you'd have an outright majority." She tilted her head slightly. "You'd have the Prime Ministership, Jon. Isn't that what you want?"

Do I tell her the truth?

I could hardly conceal it from her. Not if she were to be my wife.

"I never wanted it."

Her eyebrows rose. "I find that hard to believe."

I snorted. "Would it also surprise you to find out I'm a progressive?"

Laughter spilled from her lips, light, musical and genuine. She shook her head.

"Now I know you're joking."

I swallowed. "My Queen, I—"

"Katherine," she invited. "Or Kit. But only when we're in private or with true friends."

My heart thumped in my chest. "There are friends that aren't true?"

Her lips quirked. "Many. As you'll learn if we settle the negotiations."

"Negotiations for?"

"My hand in marriage. Come, Jon. Did you really think I would accept your proposal without question?"

My lips tipped into a grin, my body relaxing. "Never."

Her grin reappeared. "Good. Now, explain your startling claims," she said, her tone teasing.

I leaned back in my seat, somehow now firm in the knowledge that she would be mine before this dinner ended.

"What I'm about to say may shock you enough that you'll kick me out and ban me forever."

"Try me."

"Like all good stories, this one starts with a hero and a villain."

"I do like a good tale."

I hushed her, leaning forward to capture

her hand in mine, intertwining our fingers. My cock hardened when she didn't pull away, allowing me to touch the skin I had so often craved.

"Once upon a time," I began, running my thumb over the silk of her hand. "A woman found herself pregnant and alone. Her immediate family, now stout traditionalists thanks to her conservative step-father, disowned her, casting her into the streets and leaving her, and her unborn baby, to the wolves."

Kit's hand involuntarily jerked under my own, tension creeping into her limbs, her eyes blazing with outrage.

Oh, yes. You're a fierce warrior for our people.

"The woman went to her lover expecting help. But his father, a politician of the highest office, threatened to disown him as well. Unlike the fierce woman who loved both man and child, his was a paltry, weak love, and he too cast her into the world without protection."

Kit's breath caught. "She was all alone?"

"Shh, let me continue."

She grinned, squeezing my hand in encouragement.

"The woman sought refuge with her friends but they couldn't offer the long-term stability that she craved for her or her child. For two years she moved herself and her child from place to place, desperate to find somewhere to call home. It was a few days after her son's second birthday, while standing in line to receive her welfare cheque, a famous woman arrived at the centre. There was no fanfare, no cameras or reporters, just a woman seeking answers."

"Was the woman, say, five-four, brunette, with a smile that could light up the room?" Kit asked with a grin.

"Correct."

We both smiled at the description of her mother.

"So many interruptions, my Queen," I tutted.

"You'll find I'm not good at taking direction."

Desire flashed between us, awareness raising the hairs on my skin.

Perhaps not in public but in the bedroom? You'll like the directions I give.

I cleared my throat, determined to get this over with before I gave in to the aching need that had settled in my soul.

"The Queen Consort, only just beginning to show the curve of her first pregnancy, began to make her way along the line, speaking to each and every person in wait. When she reached the tired mother and her rambunctious child, the woman had struggled to curtsy, so weighed down by the weight of exhaustion and anxiety."

"'*Please,*' *said the Queen.* '*Don't worry yourself. Now, come. Let's sit and talk.*'

'*I'm sorry, my Queen, but I need my cheque to feed my little one.*'

The Queen had looked at one of her guards. '*Take her place and call us when you near the front of the line.*'"

"And with that, the Queen had taken the woman away. They sat at a local café, sipping drinks, and eating more food than the mother and her child had seen in months. They ate their fill while the Queen asked questions about their life and what the mother needed."

"'*A job,*' the woman requested. '*So I might look after my child.*'"

I cleared my throat, the next part always difficult to tell. "The Queen had considered the woman, a hand on her own stomach.

'*Do you know, the first time my child kicked was when I saw your son's face? In times gone by the elders would say that means their spirits are connected. I may not put stock in that story, but I do believe our future Monarch wishes me to help. The crown will pay for a house, and provide an allowance for as long as you need. You have my word.'"*

Kit's fingers flexed, her eyes shining with unshed tears.

"And she honoured her word. The Queen purchased the woman a house and provided her with an allowance. And every day the woman wrote to the Queen. And every day the Queen wrote back. As the babies grew, the woman found she needed a purpose. And one day, while passing the unemployment line and seeing another woman who was pregnant with a toddler in tow and nowhere to lay their heads, she stopped, and invited her home."

Kit raised her free hand to her lips, pressing them there.

"The woman wrote the Queen, as she did every day, and told her of this new living arrangement, and of her burning desire to help other women like her. And together, the women formed a plan. A charity was founded, and the women worked closely to build a foundation that would become a bedrock for those in need."

"Mallory House."

I nodded, the familiar bittersweet kick of grief and love swirled in my chest. My mother had passed from this world nearly ten years before.

"Is that the end?"

I grinned, pressing a hand to my heart. "You wound me, my Queen. Didn't you listen closely enough? We've been connected since before your birth."

She chuckled, then sobered, squeezing my hand. "I'm sorry I missed your mother's funeral. She was a magnificent woman."

"She was," I agreed. "And you were in London representing the country at Climate Change talks."

Her lips quirked. "My first appearance without my father hovering over me."

"I believe that was the event when you told the President to please stop talking over you and that you were more than capable of speaking for yourself."

She groaned, her head dropping forward and a blush tinting her cheeks. "The man was an ass. He constantly interrupted, spoke over, or tried to present his opinion as my own. 'What the Princess is trying to say is....'" She lifted her head. "I will not allow another to speak for me or our people. Do I regret my language? Perhaps. But I don't regret doing it."

Our people.

"I'm glad. It gave me a laugh in a dark time."

She squeezed my hand. "Jon, this was a

lovely story, and I'm sorry for your loss. But what does this have to do with me?"

I hesitated, wondering what my admission would cost me.

"You kicked. If not for the kick my life, my mother's life, the multiple lives their charity has assisted... it would have all been for naught." I cleared my throat. "I grew up on this tale. A simple kick that changed the course of my life. If the kick of an unborn monarch could have such a long-lasting impact, then what could a woman, fully formed and fierce, achieve?"

A small, confused frown marred her brow. "What are you saying?"

"I watched you, Kit. For years. I knew pieces of you through the letters my mother and yours shared. I knew of your habits and friendships. Your heartbreaks and daring. Long after we ceased to be playmates, I learned of you through those letters, developed a sense of the woman you were learning to be. Perhaps hero worship formed part of it, because for a good many years I had a crush on our fair princess."

She grinned, but it held a touch of reserve."

"I no longer feel that way. Now, I look at you as a woman. A woman I want to protect and love." I laughed, the sound dry and self-deprecating. "Perhaps this makes me sound like a stalker. Perhaps this obsession with you is unhealthy. But my will has been so strong for so many years that I was determined to do whatever was necessary to allow you to see me as a partner. As a potential ally."

She withdrew her hand, sitting back, her face blanking. "What are you saying?"

"The conservatives are challenged by you. They fear your spirit and the changes you want to make. They use the media and old men with loud platforms to try to silence you. In my, perhaps misguided, wisdom, I chose to sow the seeds of insurrection from within the party. I'm not a conservative, Kit. Just a very good actor."

She sucked in a breath. "You're saying you spent the last four years of your life working your way up—aggressively, I might add, the ranks of the conservatives all to... what?"

I leaned forward, our gazes meeting. "To meet you."

11

KATHERINE

Queen's Bedchamber, The Royal Palace

I paced beside the window, the inky darkness far too calm for my roiling emotions.

To meet you.

The unhinged Jonathan had left the Palace hours ago, his 'good night' accompanied by a chaste kiss to my inner wrist.

I shouldn't still feel that touch now. Shouldn't feel as if those lips had seared some unseen brand upon me.

"The man's crazy," I muttered, furious with myself. "He's a certifiable stalker. I should be glad to be rid of him."

But the heat in his eyes, the genuine

warmth and caring, the authenticity with which he'd relayed his story... it seeded doubts within me.

I reached for my phone, pressing into it the numbers he'd handed me earlier that evening.

"Hello?"

"Jon, I need to understand."

"Kit?"

I heard movement on his end, the rustling of fabric.

"Did I wake you?" I asked, suddenly aware that it was closer to morning than midnight.

"You did but that doesn't mean it isn't a welcome intrusion."

He settled while I continued to pace, that strange itchy feeling crawling under my skin.

"Now, what do you need to understand?"

"How can I be sure you're not a crazed lunatic?" The words, in no ways subtle or polished, spilled from my mouth with abandon.

He chuckled. "I knew telling you would be too much. I should have held back."

"Why didn't you?"

"Well, for one I refuse to keep secrets from the ones I love— not the important ones, anyway. Sure, birthday surprises or whatnot, but the big things? The things that truly matter? Never."

I swallowed. "Help me understand then. Are you in love with me?"

"Yes. But also no. I love what I know of you. I love your love for our people. I love your brains and sarcasm. I love your quick wit, and your generosity. I love your smile and your laugh. I love the bits of you I know, Kit. But it's hard to love someone fully when I only know the surface."

His voice dropped, the tone smoothing out. "But within me burns a desire to know more. To know everything. That's what I want."

"To control me?"

He burst out laughing, his amusement loosening the awful tension in me.

"That is an impossible feat and one I dare not even contemplate." He chuckled again. "No, I don't want to control you, Kit. I want to love you. To protect you. To give you a safe place to land."

"And being my husband is the only way to do this?"

There was a long pause down the phone line.

"No," he finally admitted. "The Prime Ministership was my original choice. It was through that office that I'd be able to further your causes."

"What changed?"

"I saw you. I felt your hand clasp mine, your breath hit my cheek as you blessed me, and I knew I wanted you. Fiercely."

"As a partner?" I asked, my heart hammering in my chest.

"As a woman. As *my* woman."

The rough desire in his voice sent shivers down my spine. My body reacted to it, a primal part of me attracted to his declaration of ownership.

This wasn't about my crown or my throne. It wasn't about the power I yielded or money and connections.

This was about me.

"Jon...."

"Should I describe what I want, my Queen? Tell you how I want to start at your neck and taste the delicate skin above your pulse? How I want to kiss and suck my way down your delicious body, worshipping at your breasts, learning the curves and peaks of your body?"

My eyes drifted closed, my body leaning against the wall to hold up my now shaky legs.

"I'd count the freckles on your skin with kisses. Tally the marks and scars with fingers that want nothing more than to know every inch of you. I'd know which trail to follow by the guide of your breath, your sighs and moans my map. I'd find your centre, Kit. Opening you to me, dipping my head to lick my way to your clit, pressing my tongue against it and teasing you until you fall apart under me, your body liquid heat against my tongue."

"Jonathan...." I tried to find the words to tell him to stop. To continue. That this isn't what I wanted. That this is exactly what I needed.

You could have this. This could be yours.

"Are you touching yourself, Kit?'"

My breath caught. "N-no."

"Why not?"

Why not?

"Are you?"

His dark chuckle had my core clenching, my body desperate and aching to be filled. "Oh yeah."

I licked dry lips, attempting to summon courage to speak around the aching need. "Tell me."

"I'm thinking of your mouth and what you said earlier tonight, that you don't follow directions well. I'm wanting to see if that would change in the bedroom. If you'd let me order you down to suck my cock. If you'd let me push between your lips. If you'd lick and suck, and swallow."

I panted, my free hand fisting the fabric of my pyjama bottoms.

"Are you touching yourself, Kit?"

I couldn't speak, could only let out a small sound of denial.

"Touch yourself, my Queen. Tell me how it feels."

My hand slowly unclenched from the fabric, sliding up to the waist band. For a second I hesitated, desperately wanting to but fearing what this meant.

"I'm doing this because I want to," I told him, annoyed that my voice sounded breathy rather than commanding.

"Of that I have no doubt."

I moved to slide my fingers beneath the waist band, my body practically begging me to offer it relief.

A knock on the door halted me.

"Your Majesty? Are you awake? There's been an accident."

I froze, my body weeping with need, my brain attempting to kick back into gear.

"Jon, I have to go."

"Wait! I—"

I hung up on him, striding across to pull it open. Victoria stood on the other side, her hair messy with sleep.

"I'm sorry to wake you, ma'am, but there's been an accident. A cruise ship has—"

"I understand. Help me dress. And hurry."

12

___

JONATHAN

Capricorn Cove

I strode into the makeshift command centre, a strange mix of anger, fear and concern roiling in my gut.

For all purposes I was still the party leader for another six hours, which meant when something went wrong during this strange election period, I was the one they called. Well, me and my opposition leader, Jane Beesley. During this caretaker period where no one party ruled, we could either elect to come to a consensus between us, or the Queen would intervene.

I suspected Kit would anyway.

"Jane," I greeted, holding my hand out to shake. Patrick trailed me, his fingers flying across his phone as he texted my deputy leader, filling her in on the situation.

"Jonathan." Jane shook my hand. "I'm sorry we're meeting like this."

"Yeah." I looked around the command centre, spotting Kit near the monitors listening intently as a man in uniform spoke. "I see our Queen is here."

"She was first on the scene and decided to take command until we could get here."

"How bad is it?"

Jane shook her head. "Cruise ship capsized off the coast. It's a small one— a domestic cruiser with about three hundred passengers and crew on board."

"Fuck."

"'Yeah. We expect it's primarily international tourists but until we can get the passenger logs, we're just waiting."

"Not that it matters. If they're in reach then we have a duty to assist."

She gave me an approving look. "In that we agree."

The next few hours flew by as decisions were made and assistance rendered.

I worked side-by-side with Jane and Kit, authorising funding, issuing emergency declarations, fielding interviews, and offering comfort to families watching.

We watched, each of us with bated breath as the navy operators cut into the belly of the ship and slowly, so freaking slowly, passengers began to emerge.

"Coffee?" Victoria asked, appearing with a cup in hand.

"Thanks." I took the offering gratefully. "What a night, huh?"

"It's certainly been illuminating, that's for sure." Her grin faded as she looked across to Kit who stood huddled with the Chief of Defence. "Can you see if she'll eat something? It's nearly lunch and she's not had a bite all day." She held out a paper bag to me.

I took it, glancing over at our Queen. "Does she do that often?"

"What? Not eat?" Victoria snorted. "Yeah, she does it all the time."

My lips pursed as I glanced Kit's way again. "Has she stopped at all since we got here?"

"No. And I doubt she will. Families will be descending soon and she'll want to be with them as much as possible."

I shook my head. "Okay. Can you do me a favour?"

"Depends, will it require murder? Cause I only do that on every third Saturday."

I grinned. "No murder, but good to know.

What I need is a small dark room where I can stow our Queen for a few minutes."

She snapped upright, giving me a jaunty salute. "On it." She pivoted on her heel, took a step, then halted, glancing over her shoulder to me. "Oh, by the way, the contract is with you. If you need a lawyer, let me know. We want to keep it hush-hush though, so appreciate if you can tell your grunt over there—" She inclined her head towards Patrick. "—to keep it quiet, that'd be great."

I nodded, then shook my head. "Wait. Sorry, contract?"

Victoria frowned, turning fully back to me. "The marriage contract. Did Katherine not tell you about it?"

I froze. "She did but I thought—" I stopped, sucking in a deep breath at the near overwhelming need to touch her, to taste her, to brand myself on Katherine.

My Queen.

She grinned, crossing her arms over her chest. "You thought?"

"Find the room, I'll get her to eat."

"Your wish, my command."

Patrick, who'd been hovering nearby, preoccupied by his mobile, looked up. "She's gone? Thank the Gods. That woman is a menace."

I grinned. "Intimidated?"

He shuddered. "More like aggrieved." He handed me the phone. "I've looked over the contract. Terms are good, clearly outlines responsibilities, if I were you, I'd sign it before she changes her mind."

"I thought you weren't speaking to me after I resigned."

He lifted one shoulder in a half-shrug. "Shit happens and now you're nearly the Prince Consort. Brother, you're gonna need me more now than ever."

Kit finished talking with the Defence Chief who moved away, leaving her standing alone for a moment, pinching the bridge of her nose.

"Gotta go. Go take a break, Pat. It's gonna be a long night."

I made my way across the centre to where Kit stood, her expression stubbornly blank.

"Here," I thrust the paperback at her. "Eat."

She took it on autopilot but didn't open the packet.

I dropped my voice and stepped closer to avoid being overheard. "Kit? You okay?"

"They've said I should be prepared for them to begin finding bodies." She lifted her face, her eyes glassy. "They're concerned the death toll could be as high as a hundred passengers."

Her words were a punch to my gut. "Fuck."

"Yeah." She pinched the bridge of her nose once more. "Have you seen Jane?"

"She's ducked out for a nap. We're taking shifts. I expect we'll be rotating in and out over the next few days."

She nodded, releasing her nose. With a deep breath she straightened her spine, squared her shoulders and looked across the command centre, her gaze searching.

"Have you seen Victoria?"

"Kit."

She looked back at me.

"Eat. It's going to be days, not hours, before this ends. You're going to need your strength."

For a moment her eyes filled, her chin wobbling. Then the emotion was gone, stripped away, hidden behind a polite nod.

"Yes, you're right. Thank you."

She moved to brush past me but I caught her hand, halting her.

"I know this isn't what you want to hear right now, but I accept the terms of your contract." I reached up, brushing a stray hair from her cheek. "But with one amendment."

"And that is?"

"You occasionally allow me to look after

you. When I asked for *akaternok ah yalonel*, I did it in the knowledge that my protection wasn't just physical. When I promise to protect someone, I mean in body and soul." I searched her face, hoping my words were penetrating. "When this is over, when you no longer need to be in the public, I'll take my Queen home and she can just be Kit—a woman who feels far too much."

Her breath caught, her face flushing slightly.

"In private you can be who you want, my Queen. Anything between us remains between us. I swear it."

She swallowed, then gave me a sharp nod. "I understand." She hesitated, glancing around before catching my hand and giving it a firm squeeze. "Thank you. I might take you up on that offer." With that, she walked away, lifting the sandwich to her lips and taking a large bite.

It was as close to a concession as she'd give me.

And despite the tragic situation, it made me feel like a king.

13

JONATHAN

Royal motorcade, on route to The Royal Palace

Katherine slumped into me, her breathing slow and even as she slumbered.

Victoria and Jane sat across from us, their own eyelids drooping.

For the last four days these women had worked tirelessly to support our country through the crisis.

In the end, three people lost their lives, Kit sitting with their families for hours, hearing their stories, letting them grieve.

While it was called a miracle that more passengers and crew hadn't died, Kit didn't see it that way. She's grieved alongside the families, feeling each death as if it had been a member of her own family.

To protect her will be a full-time job, that's for sure.

It wasn't just her body I now knew I needed to watch, it was her heart as well.

The car slowed, the smooth road turning to gravel under the tires, the car jolting a little as we drove down the back entrance to the Royal Palace.

Kit started, jerking away from me, blinking sleep from her eyes. "Are we home?"

"Nearly."

She rubbed at her face. "Okay, good. I'll need to have a look at—"

"Kit," I said softly, cupping her cheek. "You need sleep before doing anything else."

She shook her head. "The families—"

"Are likely sleeping as well, it's nearly three in the morning. Nothing cmore an happen tonight. Go and sleep. The summons and decisions can wait until tomorrow."

Her jaw clenched, her chin lifting. "You do not control me, Jon. You don't own me or order me around. I didn't give you that permission."

I loved the fire in her veins, the warrior ready to sacrifice all for her people. "And I would never ask it of you. You're exhausted, Kit. Anyone can see it. You'll have another long day tomorrow, and likely another after that. I'm suggesting you sleep so you can better deal with all your tomorrows. That's all."

The fight faded from her, her body wilting. "This doesn't mean I'm giving in."

"I never doubted it."

The car slowed to a stop, the door opening. Kit climbed out first, the rest of us following like sleepy little ducklings.

"Luke, could you please find beds for Victoria and Jane?"

"And Mr. Tuhana?" the butler asked helpfully.

She glanced back at me. "Not just yet. We have something to discuss first."

Jane and Victoria bid us good night, following the butler into the visitor wing of the palace.

"This way."

Kit led us through the quiet palace halls and down towards her private residence. There were areas of the palace where the general public could go on escorted tours during the day. Other areas where visitors and dignitaries were housed. And this wing, which was solely for the Royal Family's use.

Here, formal pictures and paintings gave way to warm candids and intimate captures.

Plants grew in pots, and flowers filled vases, all adding a lived-in feeling to the rooms.

Her hand hesitated, hovering on a door knob. "Don't judge."

I grinned. "Judge?"

She rolled her eyes, then pushed the door open, revealing her extensive private suite.

I followed her through, absently closing the door behind us, my gaze drawn to all the greenery around the room.

Plants dominated the space, turning it from a bedroom into a small jungle.

"This is...."

"A lot? A jungle? A plant hoarder's delight?" She laughed. "Go on, I've heard it all before."

"I was actually going to say incredible." I reached out a hand to touch the leaf of a giant fern. "Do you look after them?"

She nodded, gesturing at the room. "My therapist suggested green therapy as a way to deal with grief."

"Green therapy?"

"Gardening. Or looking at nature. Long story short, I'm not allowed to touch the gardens because it freaks the gardeners out and there are too many public tours and yada yada." She shrugged. "So Mother purchased me a fern and this slowly happened."

I made a mental note to purchase her plants for her birthday.

"Therapist?"

She chuckled. "Oh yes. Don't you know the Royal Family has a full suite of psychologists on staff? We're quite mad, you know."

She yawned, her jaw stretching so wide that it cracked.

"Sorry," she muttered, scrubbing a hand over her face. "I wanted to speak to you about our engagement."

"How about we sleep first?" I asked, placing a hand on her back and gently guiding her through her sitting room and toward the bed. "I'm not going anywhere."

She hesitated, glancing up at me. "Jon... you're an amazing leader. Are you sure this is what you want?" She waved a hand around absently. "You could make such a difference as Prime Minister."

I chuckled, reaching for the quilt on her bed and beginning to pull it back. "I'm sure. If anything the last few days have clarified my life's purpose."

She lifted an eyebrow. "And that is?"

"You."

14

KATHERINE

Queen's Bedchamber, The Royal Palace

I woke slowly, aware that something was different.

Oh. There's a man in my bed.

I turned slowly, looking over at Jonathan who was still fast asleep. He'd passed out on top of the covers, his arms thrown out across the bed, me snuggled into his side as he gently snuffled in his sleep.

I took the opportunity to study him, objectively finding Jonathan an attractive specimen.

He had thick biceps and a strong torso, the inky black of his hair matching that of the scruff that now decorated his face.

Something foreign and delicious unfurled in my belly as I stared at him, for once able to do so without interruption or fear of discovery.

I want him.

The thought made me uncomfortable, as if I were abusing my power by desiring someone. I'd never taken a chance on someone before. Never trusted anyone enough to allow myself to give into any desire.

Leo's first sexual partner had sold a tell-all article to a gossip column. The experience had burned Charlotte and I, providing a warning to us to choose wisely.

Charlotte may have but I'd retreated, never quite able to bring myself to the point where I'd been prepared to risk my body or my heart.

Perhaps today is the time to be a warrior.

Jon shifted, rolling onto his side, his breathing evening out once more.

My gaze dropped, narrowing in on the tenting of his boxer briefs.

Well, hello sir.

I swallowed, wanting more than anything to kiss him. To touch him. To feel him over and under me.

In me.

I sucked in a breath, rallying my spirit.

Be brave. Take a chance.

Banishing any doubts from my mind, I reached for Jon.

JONATHAN

I had to be dreaming. In my dream Kit was touching me, her fingers brushing across my cheekbones, down my neck, trailing across my chest in slow, deliberate strokes.

My cock thickened, lengthening as she dragged her nails across my nipples, then began to swirl her fingers down my side heading for my briefs.

Yes. Like that.

I'd somehow known she'd be bold, demanding. She wouldn't settle for anything but complete satisfaction— in herself and her lover.

The idea of being the man who could do that for her, who could satisfy every one of her needs left me burning. I wanted to make her ache with pleasure, to hear her cry out as we both experienced *the little death.*

"Jon? Are you awake?"

Kit's gentle voice eviscerated any lingering thought I may have had of this being a dream.

"Kit? What are you doing?"

She grinned, her hand continuing to trace the contours of my chest. "I believe it's called seducing you?"

If my cock could have hardened further, it would have, the bastard was rigid and begging for her touch.

"Seducing me? Are you sure?"

"Oh yes."

She leaned in, her lips pressing a tiny kiss to the space above my heart.

It may have been intended as a chaste kiss. Something small and innocent. But it broke my control, shattered it into a million pieces. Years of need, years of desire, poured out, forcing me to move.

I rolled up, surging over Kit, my hands pinning her down, my body pressing into her generous curves as our lips met, my tongue pressing forward until I tasted her sweetness.

"Did you touch yourself?" I grunted the words barely managing to pull back to ask her the question that had burned in my gut for days. "Were you wet on our phone call, Kit? Did my descriptions make you ache?"

She nodded, her eyes lit with desire. "Yes. To all of it."

"Fuck." I sat back, pulling her nightgown over her head, tossing it away. Her beautiful breasts were large, topped with dusky nipples.

"What did you want me to do?" I asked, her nipples peaked, awaiting my mouth. "That night. What were you begging for, Kit?"

She reached up, pulling me back down for a hard kiss, her tongue tangling with mine, our bodies grinding together in a hot, desperate embrace. Then she pulled back, grinning as she began to push my head down, guiding me to her delicious breasts. Gods-fucking-damn if it didn't make me ache for more.

I made a sound in the back of my throat. My hands running up to cup her breasts as she arched under me, a low moan escaping her.

It took all my willpower to pull away, turning my head to lave her other breast, mentally apologising for my neglect.

Perfection. Kit is perfection.

"Jon," she groaned, pushing her breasts against my mouth. "More, please."

I gave her nipple one last lick then began to shimmy down her body, my mouth and hands gliding and sucking at each new inch of skin, learning her body as I trailed down. I gently guided her legs open to reveal her to me, pressing kisses up her inner thighs, finding soft sensitive skin.

"You're beautiful, Kit."

With gentle fingers I parted her, slipping through her heat to find her sweet clit.

"Wait, Jon. You don't have to—" She cut herself off as my finger swirled around her clit, her head falling back on the bed as her hands fisted the sheets. "Oh Gods! Jon!"

I grinned, glorying in her reaction, loving the way her body responded as I pushed her to the edge then backed off, building her reaction one slow, desperate curse at a time.

"Jon." She reached up, fisting my hair, her eyes flashing dangerously. "Make me come. I need to come."

"Is that an order?"

"Yes!"

I chuckled, dropping a kiss on her abdomen. "As you wish, my Queen."

I dropped my head, shifting slightly to press my tongue against her, my fingers touching her with demanding possession.

She arched off the bed, groaning and whispering sweet demands as her hips undulated under my mouth. I built her up— this time playing with her until she shattered.

Kit bucked, legs clenching around my head, her body shaking as she came with a lusty curse.

My Queen. My woman.

I pulled away, murmuring gentle words, and stroking soft fingers across her arms and belly as she returned to herself, her body still quaking. My cock throbbed, pressing urgently against the fabric of my boxer briefs, precum dampening the material.

I need to be in her.

"There's more, if you dare."

She grinned, spreading her legs wide. "Come pleasure your Queen, warrior."

I grazed one finger up her thigh, tormenting us both with its slow glide. I bit off a curse as I pressed one finger inside her, her muscles clenching.

"Fuck," I swore, beginning to stroke into her. "So fucking wet, Kit. Fuck, you're so fucking tight."

She managed a chuckle, the sound a mixture of agony and ecstasy.

"Jon, I need more."

With a muttered groan, I worked a second finger into her tight pussy, glorying in the way her muscles stretched to accommodate me.

"Fuck I need you," I whispered against her neck, licking, and nipping and sucking at the sensitive skin. "I've waited a lifetime for you, my Kit."

She let out a little moan, her eyes drifting closed as I worked her body, my own need now a raging forest fire burning away all thoughts but one—*Mine.*

"Jonathan, I need more. I need your cock."

Her demand was one I had no choice but to answer.

I fisted the material of my briefs, shoving them down my body and kicking them away. Kit rose up slightly, watching as I moved, her gaze drawn to my cock.

"Mm." She reached out, gripping me hard, her tongue peeking out to wet her lips. "I must say I'm well pleased."

I chuckled, the sound dark and desperate. "Have you done this before?"

"Never. You?"

I shook my head. "My only sexual experiences are fisting my cock."

"I find that hard to believe."

I caught her gaze, staring into her eyes as I spoke the truth in my heart. "There's only ever been you, Kit. Never has my body burned to take another. Maybe if you'd married, I'd have felt different. But while you remained single there was hope. And that meant I couldn't even look at another without thinking of you."

Her eyes flashed, something hot and possessive burning in their depths.

"Well then." She slowly lowered herself back to the bed, spreading her arms out wide, her legs shifting to welcome me. "Come take what's yours."

I had no doubt this would hurt her but I couldn't stop. I guided my cock to her entrance, pressing against her hot centre, both of us moaning as I drew the head through the slick wet, covering myself in her need.

"Now, Jonathan. Now!"

I thrust in, freezing at her shocked hiss.

Tight. Hot. So fucking tight.

Her muscles clamped around my dick, gripping me tighter than anything I'd ever experienced. Pleasure rolled through my body like waves, my balls tightening in response.

Don't come. Don't come. Don't fucking ruin this moment by coming.

"More," Kit whispered after a moment, her body squirming under mine. "Jonathan, more."

I eased out then back in, desperate to bury myself in her, and equally as determined to prevent her further discomfort.

"I said—" She gripped my hair, tugging at my head. "—more."

With a barked laugh, I pulled back a fraction, looping one arm under her right leg, then the left, forcing them to wrap around my hips.

"Ready?" I asked, my cock gliding out of her.

"Abso-fucking-lutely."

I thrust in, fucking her tight channel, my cock branding itself on her untested muscles, shaping them to me

Beautiful. Perfect. Fucking amazing.

MINE.

"Fuck, Kit. Fuck. Fuck. Fuck. Fuck. So fucking good. You're incredible. Fuck I love you, so fucking much. So fucking tight." I lost control as she moaned my name, it fell from her lips like a curse and prayer.

"Jon, fuck, Jon. Jon. Jon. Oh Gods, Jon...."

Don't come. Don't come. Don't come.

The need to let go was near impossible to fight, yet I battled it, desperate to ensure she came first.

I dropped a hand, finding her clit, circling it once, twice. On the third pass, Kit screamed, her body clenching and bowing, her hips now bucking wildly under me as she attempted to milk my cock.

Thank fuck.

"Kit," I grunted her name as I found release, hot cum filling her as I lost myself in the woman I loved.

We slowed, panting together in the aftermath, my body crushing hers.

I tried to roll but she halted me, muttering a small protest.

"I like your weight."

And so we remained, joined together, our bodies slowly cooling.

"Oh."

She urgently wiggled under me and I rolled, coming to lay beside her.

"The first rite," she whispered, her fingers sliding down her body to her sweet pussy.

My blood caught flame as I watched her press fingers into herself, coating them with the mix of cum and desire, and the touch of her blood.

She reached for me, touching the wetness to my heart.

"Hei womulsas mia garell."

My first and only.

The words were normally reserved for wedding nights, though these days they often had the first reference dropped.

I reached down, cupping her sweet cunt.

"Hei womulsas mia garell."

In the quiet light of the morning we made the promise, those words as binding as any muttered at a wedding ceremony.

"Did you mean it?" she asked, her voice a soft whisper.

"Mean what?"

"That you love me?"

"With all my soul, my Queen."

She pressed forward, her lips finding mine.

I knew she couldn't say the words. Not yet, not when this was still so new to her and she was still so protective of her tender heart.

But she would. I had no doubt. And when she did?

I grinned, rolling us over until she was on top, sitting astride my thighs.

Kit leaned back, one eyebrow raised. "And what would you have me do, warrior?"

I fisted my rapidly hardening cock, giving it one long, vicious stroke. "Ride me, my Queen."

And glory to the Gods, she did.

16

KATHERINE

Grand Hall, The Royal Palace

Six months later

The morning of our wedding began with rain, sending Charlotte and Mother into hysterics.

I'd expected something like this from Charlotte— my sister was nothing if not flighty, but from Mother? It was quite out of character.

"How is this possible?" she moaned, staring in dismay at the rain drops as they slowly raced down the glass of the picture window.

"It's meant to clear before lunch," I said, scrolling through the forecast on my phone. "And if it rains then it shall rain and we'll get wet. It matters not."

"It matters not?" Mother repeated, her

eyebrows rising so high, I feared they would disappear into her hairline. "Kit. It's your *wedding*, how can you be so calm?"

Because all that matters is what comes after.

I couldn't quite give voice to the newborn emotions that swirled within me. They were blooming like a delicate flower, new and so ready to turn towards the sun. But it felt almost as if... as if I loved him. As if Jon and I were beginning a life together that would be beautiful and filled with joy.

Our engagement had been announced a scant few months ago. But the plans for the wedding had been in place for months prior. We'd waited, respecting the country's collective grief, and allowing them to process Jon's resignation. We'd decided to postpone until after the election, not wanting to sway the results either way.

Jane had won the election—but only by a slight margin leaving her in a minority government where the balance of power swung either way.

I couldn't say if I preferred this way of governing or not, for while it appeared fraught, the results were more robust, leading to better outcomes for my people.

My phone buzzed and I pulled it free, opening the secure app.

JON

I miss your taste.

It had been a sore point between us that we couldn't be together. Since the engagement had been announced, our every moment had been documented and monitored. The opportunities to engage in some mutual bliss had been severely curtailed. To say we were craving each other would be an understatement— I'd never been so on edge or desperate in my life.

KIT

I miss that thing you do with your tongue.

JON

Mm, so do I. I'll make sure to do it tonight.

My body clenched, heat pooling in my abdomen as tension spiralled out.

Surely the Queen should have enough power to decide not to wait for her wedding night.

I sighed, tucking my phone away and turning to focus back on the table.

Mother squirmed in her seat, checking her watch for the fifth time.

"Mother what are you—"

A harried Victoria burst in, holding a large white square box aloft.

"I found it!" she crowed, beaming at Mother.

"Found what?" I asked as Mother hurried to relieve Victoria of the package.

"Your gift, sweetheart."

She carried it away from the table towards the bedroom. I exchanged a confused glance with Charlotte, both of us following her closely. The photographer, who'd been quietly snapping pictures of us as we got ready, followed, camera pointed in our direction.

In the bedroom Mother had placed the box on the bed, stepping back to watch as I approached.

"Open it."

I gently lifted the lid to reveal soft tissue paper. I discarded the lid, then peeled back the wrapping to reveal a *merimorini*— a traditional wedding cloak.

I made a sound, my hands coming to press against my lips as I stared at the beautiful feathers and the dyed grass band that would wrap around Jon and I as we said our wedding vows.

"It has been worn by every woman who came before and will be worn by every woman who will come after you," Mother said, wrapping an arm around my waist. "It is my honour, daughter, to present this to you on your most special of days."

She turned me with gentle hands, clasping my arm to her chest, pressing her forehead against mine as she whispered the words of blessing.

May your ancestors bless you and your chosen half. May your souls merge until there is no end and no beginning. May you be at peace, and dwell in love. May your years together be long. This is our wish for you.

Mother released me, stepping back as Charlotte took her place, tears in her eyes as she too recited the blessing.

"Now come," Mother said, wiping tears from her own cheeks when Charlotte finished speaking. "Let's get you married."

17

JONATHAN

Murmuranay, City Centre

The crowd shifted, a ripple of excitement, of anticipation making its way down towards where I stood waiting for my bride.

She's coming.

Above me, the old wood creaked in the gentle breeze, the trees around us rustling, the occasional drops from this morning's rainstorm dotting my skin.

I stood barefoot on the sacred ground of the *Murmuranay*, the marriage swirls inked into the skin on my wrists.

My Queen. My forever.

Unlike many of my contemporaries who chose temporary ink, I'd sat under the needle of a tattooist that morning, prepared to declare on my skin that Katherine, my Queen, would be the only wife I would ever take.

I heard the roar of the crowd from outside the perimeter of the *Murmuranay*.

"Are you ready?" the elder, Kihana Mary, asked.

"More than ready, Kihana."

Her lips tilted up, crinkling all the wrinkles on her weathered face. "Well it looks like you won't have long to wait." She lifted a hand, holding it out towards the end of the aisle.

I turned, my heart pounding in my chest when I saw my bride standing at the end.

Somewhere, a drum began to pound, setting up the beat for the marriage chant.

Down the aisle, one bare foot stepping in front of the other, Kit walked towards me. I barely registered Leo at her side, so focussed was I on the woman I loved.

Her hair was down but for a simple crown braid. On her head sat a tiara, the jewels sparkling in the light. Her dress was simple, one made from Astipian fabric, crafted by Astipian fingers, worn by an Astipian Queen.

Leo halted her halfway down the aisle, the drums falling silent.

"Wha me rundorni ma al oinp?" Leo shouted, pounding on his chest.

Who dares marry this woman?

I stepped forward, beating on my own chest. "Ma toaeria."

This warrior.

"Mala juni meta olpola?"

What is your bride price?

I grinned, dropping to one knee, throwing my arms out wide.

"Hei grahna, hei dilsna, hei katmu."

My love, my loyalty, my life.

A mumble of surprise rippled through the guests, no doubt unused to hearing such a declaration during a royal wedding.

Leo turned back to his sister, pounding once on his chest. "Ki mar alerni ma toaeria kelipu mun?"

Do you accept this warrior, my sister?

Kit's beautiful lips curved up into a stunning smile, her joy clear as she replied in the language of our people, "Mah sagra."

I will.

Leo stepped back, pounding one fist over his heart. Behind me, the elder took up the beat, those around us joining in.

With the beating that echoed that of my heart, Kit walked to me, unassisted, unhindered. She crouched, taking my hands in hers, and guiding me to a stand, we turned to face the elder.

Kihana Mary called the ceremony to order and began the traditional blessing.

I knew I should be focussed, committing every moment of this day to memory. Instead, I searched Kit's face, determined to capture every emotion and expression.

Kihana Mary finished the blessing, commencing the ceremony.

"We meet on this sacred place to marry two lovers, uniting them under the eyes of the Gods, and on the land of our ancestors." She swept a hand out, encompassing the forest surrounding. "The *Murmuranay* is known in our culture as a meeting place. A place that straddles two times, the before and the after. It is here where births are celebrated, and deaths are mourned. And it is here where our Queen will pledge herself to the one who will be her partner, her life, the other half of her soul."

She looked beyond us to Charlotte, who stood hovering in the aisle.

"You may now cloak them in the *merimorini.*"

Charlotte moved forward as Kit and I clasped fists, stepping into each other in order to trap our arms between our bodies, our foreheads pressing tight.

"I love you," she whispered, as Charlotte settled the cloak around us.

My stomach clenched, a fierce possessive rage hitting my gut at her declaration. It was the first but I made a silent vow it wouldn't ever be the last.

"I fucking love you," I whispered back, desperately wanting to throw her down and claim her here on this hallowed ground.

"And now the vows."

We repeated our pledge to each other, declaring our love, our loyalty, our spirit to each other before the Gods, guests and all who watched on the live broadcast around the world.

"You may kiss the bride."

I captured her lips, near desperate for a taste of her. Her mouth opened and for a moment, the kiss oscillated in the space between a publicly acceptable display and a far too intimate embrace.

My cock, never one to miss an opportunity, rose to the occasion.

Suddenly grateful for the large *merimorini*, I gently pulled back, pressing my forehead to hers once more.

Applause washed over us like thunder, surging and breaking and surging once more.

"I saw your tattoos," Kit said over the noise. "You didn't have to do that."

I grinned, pressing a kiss to her lips once

again. "Of course I did. I'm yours, Kit. Today and everyday. And I want the world to know it."

We turned as one, laughing and walking down the aisle to the waiting carriage outside. Sitting in the back we made our way through the crowded streets, our people waving and laughing, celebrating this day with us as cameras followed our journey all the way to the palace.

Inside the grounds, we hurried to the library balcony, performing one last wave and kiss for the applauding crowd before disappearing back inside.

Victoria led us to a small room where we could quickly take refreshments.

"Reception now," Victoria directed, her trusty tablet held at the ready. "You'll make a brief appearance to get festivities underway. Then there will be the formal photos, then the speeches, then—"

"Victoria?"

She looked up, blinking at me. "Yes?"

"No offence," I said gently. "But get the fuck out."

Her eyes widened, flicking from me to Kit then back. "Oh no. Oh no, no, no, no, no! Please, you can't. We have a tight timeline and—"

"Sorry, Victoria. But I agree with my husband." Kit placed a hand on Victoria's lower back, gently pushing her out of the room. "We'll be out in twenty, thirty at the latest."

"Better make it forty-five," I muttered as I reached for the door.

"But—"

I shoved it close, turning the lock and making a mental note to make it up to Victoria later.

Satisfied we'd be left alone for at least a few minutes, I turned back to my wife taking a moment to bask in the magnificence of her.

"Hello, husband," she said, that familiar grin lighting her face.

"Hello, wife."

We both moved, Kit jumping up, me boosting her as our lips sought each other.

"You picked a hell of a time to declare your feelings," I growled against her lips.

"Couldn't hold it in any longer," she said between kisses. "Needed to tell you."

"Love you."

"Love you more."

I fisted her hair, crushing her against me as I turned us, pressing her against the wall.

"Say no."

She laughed, her head dipping to nip at my neck. "Never."

With a groan I fisted the skirts of her dress, shoving them up and up until she was bared to me.

"What the actual fuck, Kit?"

She chuckled, the sound breathy. "They'd never know."

She wore no underwear, her bare pussy like liquid heat as I pressed a finger against her, testing if she was ready to accept me.

"Hurry, hurry, hurry," she groaned, her body wiggling, her thick thighs clenching around my waist.

Always one to obey the command of my Queen, I shoved down my pants, fisting my cock I guided it to her entry, rubbing against her, teasing us both.

Her hips jerked against me, her wet heat coating my cock.

"Fucking hell, Kit." I dipped, positioning my cock before driving into her with rough abandon.

We both gasped, Kit stilling as I filled her, her body clenching and straining to take my thickness.

Her head fell back, a pleased hiss escaping from between her teeth. "More. Now."

"As my Queen wishes," I whispered, nipping at her earlobe.

I fucked into her, my cock hard and rough

as we both lost control of our desire, allowing it to burn bright. Kit rocked on my cock, her nails digging into my back, our love frenzied and needy, achingly desperate.

"Too fucking long," I panted, pressing kiss after kiss against her neck. "Never again."

"Never," she promised, her thighs clenching to lift her slightly before she slid back down once more. "Never, never, never."

I pressed her harder against the wall, shifting my grip on her arse to free a hand, dragging it up her body to slide between us, my thumb finding her clit. With a rough stroke, I played with her, grazing her clit in time to my thrusts.

"Oh Gods, oh...." She arched, her body bucking as she came, her pussy clutching at my cock like a fucking vice, milking me until I came, spilling deep inside her.

Mine. My Queen. My wife. Fucking mine.

It took me far longer to calm than I'd expected. The urge to mark her, to brand her to me continued to heat my blood long after I'd allowed her to slide down my body, holding her steady as she leaned against the wall, her face flushed and full of sexual satisfaction.

"Mm, I think I could get used to the occasional illicit rendezvous," she murmured, curling one hand around my neck.

"Occasional?" I barked out a laugh. "Woman, you need to check your priorities. Occasional won't cut it. I'm gonna need at least three times a day for the foreseeable future."

Her smile was slow but built, quickly becoming laughter.

"Well," she said, leaning forward to kiss me. "It's a good thing you married the Queen."

"Is it?" I asked, wrapping my arms around her, pulling her tight against me. "And why is that?"

"Cause this Queen always gets what she wants." She cupped my cheek. "And what I want is at least *four* times a day for the foreseeable future."

And she sealed that promise with a kiss.

EPILOGUE

Katherine

Munmeniar House, Summer Residence
The near future

"My turn!" The little voice demanded, waking me from my nap.

"Shh," admonished my husband. "Mummy's sleeping, remember?"

I grinned, remaining in our bed, listening for our daughter's no doubt demanding reply, inordinately pleased when she didn't disappoint.

"But I want a go!"

I reached for a pillow, stuffing it against my

mouth to suppress my giggles as I heard Jon's belaboured reply.

"And your sister had it first."

"She always gets everything first!"

My body shook with my laughter.

"That's because she was born first. You were second, and the twins will be next."

There was a beat of silence then Fiona— poor, dear, second born Fiona— decided she'd had more than enough.

"I WANT MUMMY!"

I sighed, pushing up, groaning as I struggled to get my pregnant body off the bed. "I'm coming, Princess."

A scurry of footsteps followed my words, the herd of baby elephants descending.

"Mummy!"

My girls threw themselves on the bed, chattering a mile a minute.

I nodded, listening to their excitement as I brushed at messy hair, and kissed cute little cheeks.

"Can we go for a horse ride?" our oldest, Eleanor, asked shyly.

"Not today," Jon told her, walking in to lift her up, tossing her into the air. She squealed, her legs kicking as he caught her easily, blowing raspberries on her neck.

"Tomorrow," I promised, rubbing the swell

of my belly. "You can all go and I'll follow in the car."

"Now, I believe it's dinner time munchkins. And someone needs to go bring Nanna to the table. Who's gonna go find her?"

"Me!" Fiona leapt from the bed, Eleanor following her as they dashed from the room.

Jon slumped on the bed beside me, shaking his head. "I can't believe I let you talk me into another one." He leaned over, talking directly to my stomach. "And then one turned into two. Please be meek little mice, my children. I'm not sure I have the energy to deal with another lot of hellions."

I sniggered, shoving at his head. "You love them."

"I do." He surged up to kiss me. "But I love you more. Especially today."

I chuckled, patting his cheek. "Poor baby."

"Mm, I'm going to need lots of love later." He nuzzled my neck. "Good nap?"

I nodded, leaning into him, groaning when his hand found my lower back and began massaging. "Oh, that feels amazing. Keep going."

"Is that an order?" he asked, his lips against the shell of my ear.

I chuckled, relaxing into him. "Always."

"Well then, your wish is my command, my Queen."

There was a soft knock at the door.

"Come in."

A maid entered, bopping a quick curtsy. "Ma'am? Dinner's ready."

I groaned. "Thanks, Lou. We'll be there shortly."

Jon stood up, reaching down to help me to a stand, bracing me as I swayed.

"You okay, baby?"

I nodded, closing my eyes. "Just a sore—"

Water gushed down my legs, pooling on the floor.

"Oh." I found his gaze, trying desperately not to laugh at the shocked expression on his face. "Are you telling Fiona we're not going riding tomorrow, or shall I?"

He shuddered. "You. Definitely you."

Hours later I birthed our sons into the world, both of them loudly proclaiming they'd arrived.

Jon sat on the bed beside me, one son cradled in his arms, the other in mine.

"I didn't think my heart could get any bigger," I whispered, running a finger down our son's tiny cheek. "And yet here we are."

He leaned down, pressing a kiss to my forehead. "Are you happy, Kit?"

I tipped my head back, tears shimmering in my eyes. "Blissfully so. And you?"

He tilted his head to one side. "Katherine, you've given me four children, a beautiful life, and more joy than I'd ever hoped to experience. You are all I ever wanted, my Queen. Our life is more than I could have ever hoped."

With tears wet on my cheeks, and babies in our arms, I kissed him, thankful every day that this man, this warrior, had chosen me.

And I, in my infinite wisdom, had chosen him.

Long live us.

Thank you so much for reading Kat and Jon's love story!

You can continue the entire series by checking them out on my website at www.EvieMitchell.com

*If you enter the code **EBOOK10** you can get 10% off your purchase from my website.*

ABOUT THE AUTHOR

Hey, I'm Evie Mitchell.
I'm a thirty-something romance author
(she/her/hers) living with disability. I believe in
inclusion, accessibility, and fierce romance. My
loves include steamy romance novels, my sexy
husband, our THREE sausage dogs (THE
FUR!!!), and my ever-growing collection of
book-related mugs.

As a woman with a diverse work history,
including in areas such as hospitality, retail,
emergency response, event management,
human rights, disability access, and security—
my books are filled with true stories
(bridezillas), worst-case scenarios
(malfunctioning zippers), and my favorite
tropes (one-bed).

I'm a strong proponent of #OwnVoices, and
specialize in fiercely inclusive happily ever
afters.

EvieMitchell.com
Socials: @EvieMitchellAuthor

ALSO BY EVIE MITCHELL

All Access Series

Knot My Type

Love Flushed

Darn Knit All

Larsson Siblings

Thunder Thighs

Clean Sweep

The X-List

Reality Check

The Christmas Contract

The A-List

Capricorn Cove

The Shake-up

Double the D

Muffin Top

The Mrs. Clause

New Year, Knew You

Double Breasted

As You Wish
You Sleigh Me
Meat Load
Resolution Revolution

Dogg Pack
Puppy Love
Bad English
The Frock Up
Pier Pressure
Trick or Trent
New Year's Faye

Reigning Hearts
Silent Knight

Men of Trinity Bay
Kink in the Road

Nameless Souls MC
Runner
Wrath
Ghost
Shield

Elliot Security

Rough Edge

Bleeding Edge

www.ingramcontent.com/pod-product-compliance
Lightning Source LLC
Chambersburg PA
CBHW010437170726

48283CB00011B/3247